THE PETTING ZOO

BRETT SINGER

SIMON AND SCHUSTER · NEW YORK

DESIGNED BY EVE METZ
MANUFACTURED IN THE UNITED STATES OF AMERICA

1   2   3   4   5   6   7   8   9   10
LIBRARY OF CONGRESS CATALOGING IN PUBLICATION DATA

SINGER, BRETT.
    THE PETTING ZOO.
    I. TITLE.
PZ4.S61725PE   [PS3569.I527]   813'.5'4   79–9299
ISBN 0–671–24942–8

For my grandparents,
Ethel and Mike Flaum, thriving in California,
and
Genia and I. J. Singer, alive in spirit.

The sides of wet stones cannot console me,
Nor the moss, wound with the last light.

—THEODORE ROETHKE

I

JAKE TOLD ME ONCE that when he died he wanted to be stuffed. As the mourners filed into the room, school-mates and maiden aunts, he would greet them with this tape-recorded message: "Welcome to my funeral. How do I look?"

Jake talked a lot about death, but I was a well-informed teenager, knowledgeable about suicide. I had read in innumerable newspaper columns that if a person talks about killing himself, he is unlikely to do it. Jake talked a lot about suicide. I wondered if talking about it a lot meant you were highly unlikely to do it.

One night in August when we were each twenty, Jake had hurt my feelings and I had hurt his feelings, and so he'd refused to kiss me goodnight. He was troubled that night about many things. For one, all his favorite radio programs were going off the air. Symphony Sid, a jazz disc jockey of the Big Band Era, was hanging up his headphones after twenty or thirty years. Jake tried to explain what Sid meant to him. "Listen to the words," he would say:

"Jumping with my friend, Sid, in the city. President of the deejay committee." Symphony Sid's theme song rang empty, stilted, in the front seat of the Rineharts' Buick. Jake's face sparkled with delight, then faded. Sid played the music of people who'd died too young. Charlie Parker. Billie Holiday. Bunny Berigan. I understood and didn't understand Jake's attachment to a radio program whose passing belonged to an era he had never known.

"But you can listen to records," I said.

"It's not the same," he said. "Sid is like a . . ." Jake's curls flopped onto the dashboard. His voice gave out a series of wails, low and pure as a beast's.

"It'll be okay," I said, but I didn't know what I meant. I didn't know if anything would ever be okay.

What Jake was afraid of, I now understand, was the passing of time. Whether or not one belongs to a time is a question of sensibility, a pure inclination of heart. Jake lived, while he lived at all, in a realm of dying things. Smoky things, evaporations, distillation, mist. I suspect he didn't like the generation he was born into. He was in many ways a man in retreat from his time.

But what did he want from me?

"You can listen to records," I said, untwisting and twisting his blackish curls. "You can still listen to records." We had an argument then because he wouldn't let me kiss him. He wanted, he said, to be left alone. I got angry, or pretended to anger, because I wanted out of that car and, maybe, for the first time, out of his life. What can a twenty-year-old girl, naive as an

Ann Landers item, tell a twenty-year-old boy about the passing of time?

The next day my sister discovered a piece of gauze, a piece of gauze wound many times around itself, stuck inside our mailbox. My name was written all over the gauze in red ink. Inside the gauze was an oversized Band-Aid with this message: "I'm sorry, I'm sorry, I'm sorry, I'm sorry."

I called Jake's house and his nephew's nanny answered the phone. The nanny was a seventy-year-old woman with a thick German accent.

"Mrs. Kopke," I said. "It's me, Mandy. Is Jake up?"

"No," she told me. "He's not up. I tried to wake him already. Before you called. And I can't wake him."

"Wake him again," I said. "Go in and shake him good."

Mrs. Kopke came back to the phone and she sounded as though she were crying. "I can't wake him," she said.

Although Jake and I had spent a lot of time in perfect conversational exchange with Mrs. Kopke, I imagined a language barrier. "Wake, wake," I said.

"I can't wake," Mrs. Kopke said, and then I knew she was crying and I knew that Jake was dead.

My father drove me to Jake's house and instructed me to go upstairs. If I didn't come down in five minutes, he was coming up. I rushed past the Rineharts' living-room couch where Mrs. Kopke sat, sunk into crushed velvet, wringing her hands in prayer.

I opened the door of Jake's room to find him dressed

13

in gold pajamas, and snoring as wrenchingly as a hundred-year-old man. I suspected a practical joke. Jake was capable of anything—even this. The day he took me out for my first driving lesson, he had made sure to unscrew the steering wheel. As soon as I accelerated, the wheel came off in my hands.

"Jake, goddamn it, wake up." I flung the covers off his body. I tried to lift his head. I understood in that moment the meaning of dead weight. Of gravity. Immovable objects. It took all my strength to support his body from the waist up. But his head kept flopping down. His breathing was coming though. His body was heaving and jerking crazily. Crazily, I threw myself down on top of him. It was then that my father walked in.

"He's breathing," I said.

"If you don't get off him pretty quick, he won't be breathing for long."

An odd atmosphere. My father walking in. Me on top of Jake. Me on top of the body I had lain atop so guiltily, so dreamily, so hard. My father had never even been inside the Rineharts' house. And here he was in Jake's bedroom. And Jake was wearing pajamas. Did he always wear pajamas? I had loved him for seven years. I knew everything there was to know about him, or so I thought. Everything except whether or not he wore pajamas. Or just on special occasions. Occasions when he expected company.

"Now what?" my father said.

"I don't know."

"Make him drink water." I went into the bathroom and filled a Dixie cup. I filled that two-ounce Dixie cup about four or five times before it occurred to either me or my father to find a larger cup.

My father is the kind of man who should be good in emergencies. As pragmatic as the Dow Jones. But that day in Jake's bedroom he was as inept as I. I was trying to save Jake from killing himself. My father was trying to save me from the awful passing of time.

With me holding Jake's head and waist, my father tried to lift him. But he couldn't do it.

"He weighs a ton," my father said.

"I'll call an ambulance."

"No ambulances. It's a crime, you know. We don't want the police."

I started calling doctors. I called every doctor whose name occurred to me. But no one seemed particularly interested in a comatose twenty-year-old. I called his family doctor, I called my family doctor, I called the doctors of families I didn't even know. I never actually got a doctor on the line. The nurses told me repeatedly to call an ambulance.

I decided to call Jake's father, thinking, as I did then, that the father is the strong one. I called the delicatessen in Bayside his father owned.

"Noshery . . ." It was Jake's father on the line.

"This is Mandy," I said. "Jake seems to have taken too much of his medicine. He's okay now, he's breathing and all, but he's in a coma, I think. I called Dr. Frischer, but he wouldn't come over. Who should I call?"

15

"But he didn't try to—"

"Oh no," I said. "Of course not. Just probably took a pill or two too many." The urge to defend him, to defend his parents, to defend the whole world from the idea that children don't want to live—this instinct came to me as naturally as the instinct to preserve. To preserve Jake. To preserve myself. To preserve the world we lived in—a world I really didn't know until the passing from that world of Jake, and with him, my childhood.

I first saw Jake when I was eleven years old and each of our mothers had arranged for us to join a drama club. I was a joiner, then. I took lessons every day. Tennis lessons. Drawing lessons. Flute lessons. Clarinet. My mother was straining to raise a Miss America. I was no good at any of these lessons. I was a small and uncoordinated athlete. As a musician, my intrinsic unmusicalness was less a drawback than, it turned out, my inability to spit. When the music teacher uncovered the fact that I couldn't spit, he nearly brushed tears from his rheumy blue eyes. "Well, of course you can't play a woodwind instrument if you can't spit. My wife can't spit either."

Acting wasn't physical—at least in the same sense. I landed the part of the French maid in the "fractured fairy tale" that preteen drama class put on. But Jake had dropped out of the club weeks before opening night. I remember him telling the drama teacher, the very first night of class, that he had to leave early to go to a party. It was seven-thirty on a Monday night. The drama teacher, a sharp-eyed blonde, found it strange that an eleven-year-old had a party to go to in the middle of the week.

"A party? At this hour?" Mrs. Bellman consulted her watch.

"A *real* party," Jake had said, as if that explained everything. "A party with girls."

Needless to say, I was impressed. Jake looked, I thought, like Paul McCartney. He'd introduced himself that first night as "Lightbeam" Rinehart. He said they called him that because he was so fast on his feet. He and Ronald Cooper—a boy I ended up with at a *real* party a year later as a result of a trade-in—Jake and Ronald Cooper had done an improvisation that first night from *West Side Story*.

I have no idea anymore what it feels like to be eleven years old and in love. I am not at all sure if the name "Lightbeam" occurred to me then as romantic or silly. But eleven years old, unaggressive, fragile, relegated with all the clamorous certainty of second-best to the role of walk-on maid, I decided two things about my life that September night: Someday I would be the star of the show; and someday I would wake up and be Mrs. Lightbeam Rinehart.

That image of Jake, small and dancing, dancing the improvised battle of the war between Sharks and Jets, is

17

an image that stayed with me during the nine or so months before I saw him again. During those nine months, I have started wearing nylon stockings. I wear the smallest size nylon stockings they make and they bunch around my ankles in thicknesses of five or six folds. But that is okay because all the girls' stockings do not fit. It is practically the style.

I am wearing stockings for the first time that second time I see Jake. Daniel Webster Junior High School is holding an orientation assembly for all graduating sixth-graders. I am wearing stockings for the first time and I am wearing a brassiere for at least the hundredth. I am shorter than everyone in the class so I get to walk right behind Mrs. Kerner. I like being near the teacher because the teacher is wild about me and my classmates feel just so-so. I am friends with a lot of the popular girls, but they don't really like me. I am aware they don't like me, but it doesn't matter that much. It only matters to be popular, being liked has nothing to do with it.

The sixth-graders are marching towards junior high school. We haven't graduated yet. We will graduate in two weeks and then will begin all the rounds of parties to which the girls invite the boys. The most important graduation party will be Janie Moscoff's. Janie's mother, someone has told me, approves of kissing games. Once, at a party, the year before, Janie Moscoff's mother *taught* everyone how to play "Cocktails." The emcee calls out the name of a drink, and if you've been assigned the same drink as a boy, then you have to kiss him. I imagine Mrs. Moscoff, her spike heels piercing green lawn, calling out "champagne," and me having to kiss Larry Packer on the mouth.

It is two weeks before Janie Moscoff's party, to which I've already been invited. Two weeks before Larry Packer trades me—right in the middle of the kissing games—to Ronald Cooper. Because it is two weeks before I am publicly humiliated by a real boy in front of practically everyone I know, I am feeling rather dizzy and full of myself. I travel the path of Mrs. Kerner's broken veins, up the back of her knee and into the underneath of her skirt where I imagine she wears three pairs of bloomers, a panty girdle, two kinds of slip. Mrs. Kerner has only one boobie. The other one was surgically removed.

We are led into the auditorium by an officious boy of fifteen. He introduces himself as the president of the Student Council. He stands a head taller than all the boys in my sixth-grade class, except for Fred Muller.

(Fred has been erasing blackboards and pulling down shades since second grade. Fred was a boy of considerable intelligence, but nowadays he probably works as a janitor.)

Bobby Kovac, the president of the Student Council, pats Janie Moscoff on the head. "Hey, Moscoff," he says. A loud whispering goes up among the graduating sixth graders. It takes only a few seconds to find out that Janie's older sister, an eighth-grader and a cheerleader, is practically engaged to Bobby Kovac. I shudder to think I am about to go off to a school where people roam the halls, practically engaged. I wonder if the popular kids all call each other by their last names? I turn to my friend Debra. "Hey, Gerber," I say. Debra laughs and flashes me an understanding look. In junior high, Debra becomes famous for her "doody roll." A doody roll is a much-discussed failure of the ends of the hair to flip like they're supposed to. In a perfect flip, the ends of the hair—the flip *per se*—stand about an inch away from the back of the head. In a doody roll, the hair ends curl back onto themselves to form a crescent-shaped worm.

Debra Gerber's doody roll is not yet famous. These days, practically anyone will sit down at lunch with her.

Seated in the junior high school auditorium, I see him again. He is sitting off to the back with the kids entering Webster from private elementary schools. I am about to go to a *real* party, I want to tell him. But I am thrilled to know he will be roaming the halls as soon as summer is over. Roaming the halls with me and the other graduating sixth-graders. Roaming the halls with cheerleaders, Student Council presidents, honor patrols, prom queens, the occasional fiancée.

Downstairs, Mrs. Kopke refuses to answer the door. Hearing the knock all the way upstairs, I make my way to the living room and let in the carpet installers, three burly boys, just older than myself. I let my father know the carpet men are there. He goes down, and explaining nothing, not even that Jake is alive, not even that Jake is not a victim we have sedated with memory drugs, my father goes down and fetches two of the carpet men.

They carry Jake like a roll of broadloom into my family's car.

I rush back up to Jake's bedroom. I feel like I'm moving out of a house and have come to examine bare baseboards, to whisper good-bys to wall plugs. Part of me wants to curl into the warm spot his body has left in the bed. Curl up with his leftover sleep and, maybe, never wake up. I touch the sheets. They are royal blue, boys' sheets, warm and slightly dampish. Next to the bed is a volume of Robert Benchley and an empty sample bottle of pills. I read the label off the medicine bottle. I am gathering evidence. But against whom?

My father comes back upstairs. "He's in the car," he says. "I'll take him now. To the hospital. You wait for Mrs. Rinehart."

"Homestead Hospital?" I ask. My father's eyes look me over. But what is he looking for?

"Take this," I say, handing him the empty sample. "It's Triavil," I say. "This is what he took."

The phone rings and I answer it. "Mandy, where is he?" Mrs. Rhinehart says she is leaving work now and will meet me at the house. "It's okay, dear. Manny says he's breathing. He's breathing, darling, isn't he?"

"Of course he's breathing," I say.

The phone rings and this time it's Jake's psychiatrist. The mysterious Saturday afternoon appointment I had thought for years was a girl.

21

"This is Mandy. Jake's girlfriend. You probably know about me."

"Yes. Well, tell Mrs. Rinehart to call me again. I'm sorry I missed her. I'll be here all afternoon."

"Is it *my* fault?" I ask.

"I don't know. His grandfather's death was very hard on him. He reacted unusually, I think."

"Does he hate me?" I ask.

"I don't know."

"All his favorite radio programs are going off the air, you know. One after another." Like flies, I want to say.

There is a long, kinetic stillness. In the distance, on a crossed connection, I can hear the voice of a Puerto Rican woman arguing.

"Well, Mandy, we can only hope he won't repeat this experience. I think we can help him though. I think we can all help him find some reason to like himself more. Now, I know you're upset, but I have a patient. So tell Mrs. Rinehart—"

"What if Mrs. Rinehart has a car crash on the way back from work? What if—"

"These things happen," he says.

Replacing the phone, I realize what Dr. Nold means. He doesn't mean that car crashes happen. He means that twenty-year-old boys try to suicide all the time. I had wanted more from Dr. Nold. I had wanted him to call this thing by a name. I had wanted him to tell me everything Jake ever said about me, starting with sixth grade. I wanted him to call this thing what it is—Jake wants to die. Jake wants to be a cadaver. Jake wants to

22

be a skeleton. A corpse. A stiff. A dead person. Dead. I want to be a poet or maybe a college professor. And Jake wants to be a dead person. Can this marriage be saved?

Mrs. Rinehart is suddenly there. Her presence startles me and I leap up from Jake's bed. Instinctively she inches to the bed and her hand, like mine before it, rests in a small boy-shaped well where the sheet is darker, and dampish. Our eyes catch and we look, long, into each other's face. We are each somehow alone in this. I am his lover, his girlfriend, his Mandy. For years, he was cold to me and I chased him. I would walk my family's giddy bulldog down past the Little League field and onto Pennington Road where they lived. I would ring the bell and Mrs. Rinehart would answer the door. Upstairs, then, the light would go off in Jake's attic room. And Mrs. Rinehart would look at me, her eyes pleading forgiveness, and tell me no, that Jackie wasn't home. All those years I had known, though, that she was rooting for me; that she, his pretty, indulgent mother, was on my side.

Once, at fifteen, on one of these trips, walking my dog, I told her I loved him, that one day I'd marry him. And even though she knew that Jake avoided me, even though we both knew together why the light in the Rineharts' attic went out as soon as I appeared, and even though she lied to me—a mother's sometime duty —she let me know with the look in her eyes—maternal, mammalian, moist—that she liked me, she approved.

* * *

The look we exchange now is different, more dangerous. I am his lover. She is Ma. We are not rivals, but we
aren't quite allies. Death, and closeness to it, changes
even the most assured of connections. What we see in
each other's eyes is guilt, and the fear of blame. "Poor
Mrs. Rinehart," I say as I touch my hand to her hand,
both hands alive in the once-warm place where Jake
sleeps at night.

As we drive to Homestead Hospital, I fantasize about
funerals. In the ninth grade I went to a funeral for two
sisters and their cousin. Three blood-connected girls in
three mahogany coffins. White flowers everywhere.
Three virgins killed through a failure to yield right of
way. I knew one of the dead girls, but only very slightly.
But I had been determined to go to the funeral. Jake
had been contemptuous at what he took to be false manners. He and Mary Russo had actually kidded around
together in homeroom, and *he* wasn't going. Why was I
going to a funeral for someone I barely knew? I didn't
know myself until that day in November when I
watched them lower Jake's body into the yielding earth.
An overachiever all my life, I wanted to be good at
funerals. With Mary Russo, I'd only been practicing. I
wanted to be ready for the real thing.

"Hmm?" I say.
"A tissue," Mrs. Rinehart says. "Could you hand me
one of those tissues?"
"I'm sorry. I was spacing out."

24

"You were——"

"I was thinking. About Jake. About how he'll feel when he wakes up."

"He'll feel stupid, I hope," she says. "He'll . . ." Mrs. Rinehart starts crying.

"Do you want me to drive?" I ask.

We round the parking lot together, arms touching lightly. When we get to the entrance, Jake's mother stops, takes off her glasses, and looks at me in the full light of the sun. "Let's both behave ourselves," she says. "Neither of us are allowed to cry."

Outside the emergency room, my father is sitting with Mr. Rinehart.

"Yeah, the liquor carries the business," Manny Rinehart says. My father nods his head in sympathy. I introduce Mrs. Rinehart to my father, who's wearing a purple sweatshirt. There are grass stains on his white pants and his jaw is whiskery. I wonder if Mrs. Rinehart knows he is a painter; I wonder if she finds my family a little bit outré.

Jake and I have been going out for seven years, seven years on and off, but our parents have never met. I rehearsed those meetings endlessly in my imagination. The parents are gathered at dinner, our house or theirs. They are discussing the arrangements for Jake and Mandy's wedding. My mother asks Mrs. Rinehart where she would go for rented chairs. Mrs. Rinehart asks my mother to pass the London broil, and tells her about a rental emporium where you pay less for velvet than you'd normally pay for vinyl. My father looks into Manny Rinehart's face. He is looking for his future. Will his grandchildren inherit the hook in Manny's nose? Will they develop his gift for the Market? Will Jake and Mandy raise a horde of midgets? None of the parents is taller than five feet seven.

"I've always wanted to meet you." Mrs. Rinehart takes my father's hand, forgets herself, doesn't let go. My father squeezes hers, a squat, dimpled hand with short, squared-off nails. Mrs. Rinehart remembers her hand, smiles apologetically, retrieves it. Fluorescent light flickers.

My father motions me to sit down. Let the parents confer alone. They wheel a body past us then. The man's face is blue. I am sure he is dead.

Once, my cousin's dog had puppies. There were two puppies at first, but one got sick right away. My cousin's boyfriend and I drove fifteen miles to the cat and dog hospital. While Scott drove, I held the puppy, wrapped in a nightgown, hugged to my chest. I felt a throb before we were even out of the driveway, a throb I knew was mortal. But I let Scott drive the fifteen miles, would have let him drive fifty. It was easier to hold a dead puppy than a dying one. It was easier to hold a dead puppy in peach-colored flannel than to have to say that word.

Mrs. Rinehart gestures to me from the door of the emergency room. As I walk past the stretcher, the ambulance attendant lifts one arm of the blue-faced man, lets it drop weightily. "This party's over," the attendant says.

"Jackie's over there." Mrs. Rinehart points. In her voice there is something strange—is it pride? What can I do? Wave? Does Mrs. Rinehart want me to go up and look? The bottles and the steel and the smells all make me sick. I can't look. Tell her not to make me look.

My father leaves me at the hospital. Mr. Rinehart decides to go back to the deli. There is nothing for us to do but wait till Jake comes out of it.

Annette Rinehart pulls Jake's Blue Cross card out from her card case.
"And where was he born?" the official woman asks. This time she looks at me.
"He was born in this very hospital. He's still only a baby," she says. Jake has almost come full circle.

I think of his baby pictures. I own a baby picture myself, though Jake doesn't know about it. It was given to me by Kerri Mandel. Kerri and Jake were babies together. Kerri called Mrs. Rinehart "Auntie Nettie," and Jake called Mrs. Mandel "Auntie Lanie."

Kerri sat behind me in Media in high school. She told me about the first time Jake ever kissed a girl and whom. She told me about how Jake had been the first boy anybody knew to shave; she lowered her voice and told me he'd been the first boy for blocks with hair. They used to play doctor together. They used to pull down each other's pants and promise not to tell their mothers. Only Jake would always tell. And once he told Kerri he couldn't eat dinner at her house that night because his mother was making chuck roast and Chuck was his brother's name.

In the intensive care waiting room, a fat woman is knitting squares. I tell Mrs. Rinehart the story about the chuck roast. She laughs and tells me Jake hated to eat anywhere but home. He didn't like to sleep over at other kids' houses either. Sometimes, she says, he'd make an arrangement to sleep at someone's house, then tell her to call there and order him home at once.

"He was always a special child," she says. By special she means difficult. And difficult means disturbed. Special, difficult, disturbed. All euphemisms that apply fairly and charitably to children. Children with crossed eyes, children with stutters, children who walk with braces or don't walk at all. Children who never speak. Children in India, their bodies pear-shaped with hunger, their eyes bugging out into a gaze as lifeless as pud-

28

ding. What happens to these special children? There is no such thing as a special adult.

What is wrong with Jake? There are secrets everywhere. On a bus, once, someone tells me how he hid at day camp and couldn't be found until they went to burn the trash. When they found him, an undersized eight-year-old, inside the incinerator, they asked him why he was in there. He said he wanted to be burned up.

There are other stories. Stories about his love affair with a thin, gray-faced girl who was afraid of everything. She was in the "Special Services" classes all through high school. No one ever explained what the Special Services classes were. Judging from who walked in and out of their annex classroom, it was impossible to tell. Some of the kids were obviously sick. I would meet them in gym classes or driver's ed. One such girl was the thin girl, afraid of everything.

We would be sitting around on the sidelines, letting the athletic girls fill out the mercifully meager teams of six. There on the sidelines, we unathletic types talked incessantly about sex. Who was and who wasn't. How to do it so it doesn't hurt. The thin girl would gravitate towards me, as many misfits did when I was sixteen and kind. "I'm scared," she would whisper in a voice as thin as her wrist. "I'm scared."

"Tell Mrs. Rossotti you want to go to the nurse."

"I can't. The nurse wants to kill me."

The thin girl would tremble and shake and I would try to reassure her that the gym walls were intact, that her gym suit and mine were clean, that she wouldn't have to play, because there were strange eager girls, tall girls with tall boyfriends, who were dying to be on one team or another. Her name was Reva and she terrified me.

But there were other types of kids in the Special Services classes. Kids who came to school so high on LSD, it was much mellower to sit in the Special Services annex and make collages out of *Time* magazine than go to class. In the sixties, there were more "special" adolescents than not.

A friend of a friend was a special hippie. And she told my friend that Reva Busch had admitted in that morning's t-group that she was sleeping with Jake, that she was in love with him. Word got around and Jake consistently denied it, told people Reva was crazy. And only Jake and Reva and, I, many years later, knew it was all true.

"I shouldn't have had him, maybe," Mrs. Rinehart says. "I was thirty-eight when I had him, and probably I was too old. Maybe God is punishing me for being selfish."

"Of course you should have had him," I say. "He loves you so much."

"He's always been a wonderful son. He can always make me laugh. Why can't *I* make *him* laugh?"

"You make him laugh," I say.

"Ah, c'mon, when did I ever make him laugh?"

We are bantering now. And it is so much easier than talking.

By the rules of the intensive care unit, we are allowed one five-minute visit every hour. That is, Mrs. Rinehart is allowed. I am not an immediate relative and am allowed nothing. But Mrs. Rinehart says I'm his sister, and so they let me in.

I have visited Jake twice. He is now wearing restrainers. When the nurse inserted the catheter into his penis, he bit her. I think it is hysterically funny that Jake has bitten a nurse. I am already working on my routine—my routine for when Jake revives. When I tell him he has bitten a nurse, he is bound to laugh. If I can make him laugh, I can make him live. I can make him live.

Jake could make anyone laugh. To know him was to be delighted by him, to know him was to slap your knee. To know him was to be the receiving end of a long series of jokes.

The comedy acts I especially loved were the ones through which he manipulated his mother. Annette Rinehart was her son's best straight man. When she was annoyed at him—for spending his allowance on a twenty-dollar gorilla mask, for staying out all night in Greenwich Village and getting propositioned by a man, for making love to me while his father mowed the Saturday lawn and she moved the garden furniture—then Jake would win her back with a joke.

Once he went upstairs to her room and took me with

him. We sat on the edge of the comforter where she lay in bed reading James Michener. "Mother," he had said, "I hate to have to tell you this. But Lana Mandel told me you were spotted in the A&P wearing nothing but panty hose." There was such a pure light of love in their faces, I sometimes felt I could see that love, a dotted line of radiant motes, a string of holy spittle.

"No," Mrs. Rinehart would say, winking at me. "That wasn't me in the A&P. I would never go to the market without my pants on."

"A heart attack," the fat woman says, shaking auburn curls. The fat woman and her props have taken over the entire waiting room. There are pieces of afghan everywhere: yellow squares are piled up on the linoleum, rosy squares sit on top of *McCalls*, baby-blue squares slide off the armrest and into Mrs. Rinehart's lap.

"A heart attack," the fat woman says.

Mrs. Rinehart smiles.

"What's yours?" the fat woman asks.

Mrs. Rinehart looks down at her calves. She has nice legs for a short person.

"It's okay if you don't want to say. Mine's a heart attack. Forty years," the fat woman says, purling. "Forty years and then I find him sitting on the can . . ."

Laughing is the heart's own song, Jake had taught me that. But what happens when the funny bone splinters into gray meal? What happens when the world grows so grim there isn't a laugh to stand on? In playing to the world, Jake was playing to an increasingly hostile audi-

32

ence. The hecklers were no more the blowzy drunks who are actually nice guys with a gripe. They weren't the nay-sayers you could turn upside down to your own advantage. The stage was getting smaller, the audience was growing older, the crowd was breeding a whole new mutant of adversary—guys who would sell your whole childhood for a hot tip on the horses, for a good piece, for a pound of pot. Suddenly all the nice people had moved away from the world or were dead. The people in the audience who'd loved you, coddled you, who'd talked with your diaper pins sticking out of their mouths, even these people were lying to you every chance they got.

Even that skinny nervous girl, Mandy, who stared at you for two whole years before you even met her, even she was a no-good, lying, betraying infidel. And she wasn't getting any younger or sweeter. She was practically grown up now, and she didn't belong to you, even though even she would admit you'd practically invented her. She had all kinds of ideas these days that frightened you. She wanted to be up there on the stage herself, not out there in the audience. She wanted equal time. And even though she looked kind of pretty, delectable even, in the soft green glow of the limelight, she would ad-lib too much, change the script, kiss other people, call you the wrong name when you woke her up in the middle of the night. Sure she was still the best fan a man could find, a regular pompon girl with her sonnets all about you and stuff, but maybe you needed a different type—one who wasn't so pretty, maybe. One who didn't love you so much it made you cry.

*   *   *

The intensive care nurse motions to Mrs. Rinehart. "That son of yours—the one with the restrainers. What's he like—when he's regular, I mean—is he full of anger?"

"Oh no. Jackie is very gentle."

The nurse looks at me as if she is thinking "Sure."

"Can I go in now? To see him?" I ask.

"Oh no. Only immediate family."

"I'm his sister," I say. I feel illegitimate, I feel like a bag lady smuggled into Bonwit's. I look at the nurse so pleadingly, she relents.

"We oughta check IDs around here," she says.

Inside the intensive care unit, everyone is dying except for Jake. Everyone else is old. Everyone else has had a fair shake. No one else is young enough to have been born two flights up in the new maternity annex. No one else is young enough to receive kisses as quick and sweet as a whiff of guava jelly. I kiss his wrists, his forehead, his neck. He grunts like an unfriendly dog. A thick film of mucus covers his lips. As penance, I kiss these lips wetly. I clean him like a mother baboon.

"All right, you over there. The sister. What are you trying to do? Give these old men another stroke on top of the one they've got?"

As I leave his bedside, he mutters something. If this were a practical joke, Jake would be mumbling "Rosebud."

34

* * *

I go home for dinner and it's the first time I see my mother. I am a little afraid of my mother's sympathy. As soon as I see her, I start to cry. We make jokes and cry together. She decides it is her mother's duty to go to the hospital. To sit with Mrs. Rinehart and cry and be mothers together.

"No, Ma. You make everybody cry."

"I won't cry. I promise."

I introduce my mother to Mrs. Rinehart, who is waiting outside to drive us to the hospital.

"Mrs. Rinehart, this is my mother, Sonia."

My mother looks at Annette Rinehart and then all three of us start to cry.

"No crying allowed, Mrs. Charney. Mandy and I already decided we aren't going to cry."

My mother looks like a child who has had her wrist slapped. "I'm sorry," she says.

What Annette Rinehart doesn't know is that my mother and I love to make each other cry. It is our most intense private communion. Like Jake telling her she was seen naked in shopping centers.

Jake is still comatose. But his father, during his six o'clock visit, heard him mutter something. "What did he say?" I ask Mrs. Rinehart.

"I don't know if I should tell you. These things don't make real sense. People shouldn't pay attention."

Two skinny old ladies sit in the corner. They look like sisters and seem terribly chipper for the intensive care waiting room. A perfumy cloud seems to emanate from around their heads—the smell of women gone old. Cracked powder, used-up violets, persecuted insteps. The women are giggling. Perhaps they are waiting out the death of a fortune, perhaps they are on the brink of becoming filthy rich.

"Tell me anyway," I say. "What Jake said in the coma."

"He said, 'Chuck, why are you locking me out?' " Tears now. She's gone and broken the no-crying rule. Quickly she regains composure and explains to my mother that Chuck is her middle son.

"The psychiatrist?" my mother asks.

"No, no, the stockbroker. The middle boy. The doctors say Jackie feels inadequate because his brothers are successful. I've told him a million times, I only want him to be happy. If he doesn't want to go to school, he doesn't have to go. But he feels guilty. I've done everything. If he wants to be a washboard player, it's okay. It's okay. I don't care. He can dig ditches."

I believe Mrs. Rinehart when she says she only wants for Jake to be happy. There is no double bind there, no cutting edge of guilt. And yet they both feel guilty. She feels guilty that he wants to die. He feels guilty that he doesn't want to live. He is a spoiled child—I have never thought otherwise. He gets secret money from both parents, he has never worked a day in his life. He comes home at odd hours, and doesn't let them know where he's been. He takes me to bed, in the afternoons, on the permanent press sheets his mother irons anyway. Just in case, may the evil eye spare us, nothing is permanent in this world—neither sheets nor money nor love.

"Chuck, don't lock me out." That one sleep-born sentence carries the guilt of the ages. What really makes parents despair is not a child stabbing his own mother with the grapefruit knife, but a child stabbing his brother. It is Biblical, this passion for loyalty between brothers. And on his gray-blue forehead Jake now wears that mark. Or is it Chuck who wears it? Who betrayed whom?

Chuck has been Jake's idol as long as I have known him. It was Chuck who practiced long hours in front of the mirror till he mastered the tongue tricks he taught to Baby Jake. It was Chuck who gave Jake his politics and his first taste of sex when the younger brother discovered him in an upstairs bedroom with a chesty Freedom Rider. It was Chuck who'd turned Jake on to Jean Shepherd, Paul Krassner, Symphony Sid.

I had only met Chuck a few times at this point that Jake lay comatose, mumbling his name. I liked him and found him intelligent, but what I really thought had to do with this advice lifted from Jake's adolescence: "Don't expect it to be too great. You'll find out soon enough you really prefer doing it *without* the girl." So Chuck represented a kind of odd challenge to me, a challenge I didn't understand. I needed to prove myself in his eyes, I needed to prove to him that Jake would rather do it with *me* around. When we visited Chuck and his wife, Sandy, I found myself trying to attract his erotic attention. I wanted him to be proud of Jake—to know that his protégé had succeeded where he had failed.

But had Chuck failed? He was, now, as Jake lay breathing through a long series of tubes, a Harvard Business School graduate working for an important brokerage. In his living room there hung a Picasso. His wife had just birthed a baby boy, plump and happy and blue-eyed. Who could call him a failure?

Jake hated Chuck in his secret heart. Hated the quick turnabout his brother had made from Freedom Rider to sly stockbroker. Jake was only thirteen when Chuck married Sandy, a rich, mixed-up girl who supposedly turned him straight.

Chuck, the three evenings I'd spent in his living room, had narrated the events leading up to his marriage. He had told the story of his fateful meeting with the then-Sandy Greenwald in Junior's as if the meeting equaled some Yalta Conference, as if it were the life of a great man that was being considered. That moment he sat down at the table in Junior's and ordered baked apple, he wanted me to believe, something had happened. History had occurred. As far as the objective listener could tell, a sometime SNCC-organizer, philosophy graduate school dropout, listener to jazz, had found a nice Jewish girl and decided to clean up his only slightly dingy act. So what? Why did he tell the story so many times?

Chuck and Sandy had gotten married at the Pierre, and although all the other males in the wedding party were ordered to wear, and wore, silk top hats, Jake wasn't allowed to. Beyond this grievance that Jake held against Sandy and against all the Greenwalds in general, held this very moment that his grayish form struggled against leather restrainers, I was never quite sure what Chuck had done to betray Jake so mightily. But betrayal had been done. His marriage to Sandy, in Jake's murky unconscious, signified some breach of trust, some failure of commitment. Chuck had stopped undressing method actresses, had stopped writing night letters to the Warren Commission, had stopped practicing contortions in the mirror above the bathroom sink that both boys shared.

I imagine Chuck at the mirror making the face of a monkey. His face is half-covered with Burma-Shave, he is wearing University of Rochester gym shorts. Jake stares at the black stubble glued to the sink with blue-white foam. He watches, fascinated, as one solitary bristle dances down the drain.

"You shave yet, Jackie?"

"I've been shaving since sixth grade. 'Cause I have to."

"Shaving. Sex. It's all a disappointment, pal. Don't look forward to any of it. Stay young and don't marry anybody."

"Are you marrying anybody?" Jake's voice squeaks badly. He doesn't think he can bear the rightful answer to the question.

"Here's the story," Chuck says. "Either I go over there in thirty minutes, tell Sandy I'll marry her, marry her in the fucking Plaza Hotel, make babies, go to business school, hang out with rich people, get myself elected the first Jewish president—or else I stay home and dress up like Dracula and chase you around the living room."

"Chase me around the living room," Jake says bravely. His eyes are starting to tear, and if his big brother sees him cry, they'll never be secret brothers again.

"I want to," Chuck says. "Don't tell Mom. But I want to stay here and I don't want to be the first Jewish president. Sandy's a great girl. They're all great girls. But don't marry anybody. Or else marry a Black chick."

"Then why are you getting married?" Jake asks. "Why? Why? Why? Why?" His tone becomes hysterical and he begins to cry openly.

"We'll still be pals," Chuck says. "We'll still be secret brothers."

"You'll have to stop reading *Playboy*. You'll have to eat everything she cooks. . . ." Jake searches his thirteen-year-old mind for the worst imaginable domestic tyranny. "You'll have to . . . eat stewed tomatoes," he says. Jake starts trembling and Chuck grabs him around the waist. Chuck lifts his brother off the floor and onto his shoulders.

"Tell the kid in the mirror he's a Communist sympathizer," Chuck says to his brother.

"But I can't sell him out," Jake says. "He's my buddy."

"Tell the kid in the mirror he kissed Joe McCarthy on the lips."

Jake has no idea who Joe McCarthy is, but he starts

40

to laugh uncontrollably. He is sure he has convinced Chuck that marriage would be traitorous.

"Tell the kid in the mirror that as secretary of defense to the first Jewish president, it's his job to forget everything I told him and to beat up anybody who says Sandy Greenwald isn't beautiful."

At the mention of Sandy's name, Jake's face droops. "Don't do it," Jake says. "Don't marry her. Please don't marry her."

Chuck looks into the mirror. Perhaps he sees a younger version of himself. Perhaps he sees a better version. Perhaps he sees nothing except his smallish, sensitive brother, his protégé, his better half, his greatest, his only fan.

"Remember everything I taught you," Chuck says as he replaces his brother on the jacquard tile. "And it really isn't so bad—marriage. Free meals. All the nooky you want. An instant fan club with your own secretary."

"But what about me?" Jake says. "When you leave, I'll be here all alone. I'll have to walk Girlie every day. If the bathtub is dirty, I'll be the only suspect. . . . What about me?"

"What *about* you?" Annette Rinehart says, entering the bathroom with the dispatch of a Gestapo, straightening towels, striking out with a sponge. "You better put something else on, Chuck. The Greenwalds are here. The in-laws."

"In-laws?" Jake is struck dumb. He knocks his fist into his forehead to dramatize his shock. Chuck leaves the room to change, and his mother, her form bent over the bathtub with a scouring rag, cannot see him. He knocks himself in the forehead again and again and again. His reflection in the mirror is taunting. How much can you take, kid? the reflection wants to know.

The intensive care nurse comes in and whispers to Mrs. Rinehart. Her face brightens and instinctively she squeezes my mother's hand.

"Can I see him?" I ask the nurse.

"Who are you?" she asks.

"I'm his sister."

"No you're not," the nurse says.

"Let her see him," Mrs. Rinehart says. "She loves him. He calls her his wife. They're in love."

At the mention of the word love, the nurse screws up her face. "It's probably your fault he's in here in the first place."

My mother lurches in disbelief. Mrs. Rinehart looks stunned. The nurse looks from mother to mother, and then at me. "Plenty of people in love drive each other to worse. Don't you upset him," she says.

In a matter of seconds, her voice has softened from rule-worshipping bureaucrat to world-hardened saloon girl. She makes an incongruous figure in this surburban drama of mothers and sons, children and guilt. Her hair is the same shade of red as Belle Watling's, her uniform stretches unprofessionally across heavy breasts. Suddenly I realize she is an indicator, a voice. My mother doesn't know about Jake and me. His mother doesn't know either. They don't know the gritty, bloody truth of our love. They can't see the central heat, the passion, the lustfulness that strikes the aggrieved lover the moment that danger strikes. They aren't aroused, as I am, by the smell of his closeness-to-death. They aren't thinking, as I am, of those moments when he shook his head with the frenzy of affirmation: "I am, I am, I am, I am," his curly, sweaty head now buried between my breasts.

The nurse knows about lovers. The danger of love, its cutting edge as sharp as sea creatures' teeth. She has been tough with me, and through this toughness, realistic. While my mother and Jake's mother are thinking mother-thoughts, are thinking all the way back down the blue-and-pink birth canal to the moment of first fetal life, I am thinking of Jake's chest—the way it heaves when he kisses me. My love is not pure.

I didn't wake up from sleep to feed him, I didn't strain his carrots *twice* so that he wouldn't choke. I didn't polish his *tooshie* with Baby Magic and kisses. I am guilty of loving him with anger, I am guilty of loving him with ambivalence, I am guilty of being afraid to love a man who cries so easily. I am guilty of looking for back doors. I am guilty of wanting out. I am guilty of loving him too little and too much, too long and too complexly. I am guilty of demanding every molecule of his love in one breath and betraying him in the next breath with his friend in a garage. I am guilty of all the ambiguity of chosen love, its destructiveness and dark side. The nurse does not look at Jake through the mother's nursery-eye-view. Like me, she sees a man who somebody has broken.

As Jake snorts, a tube becomes dislodged from his nostril. There is nothing to do but stare at his scowling face, his delicate violet-veined pallor, his thick mustache, the soft, childish chin. I want him to say something. I want him to sense it is me, Mandy, by his bedside. I want him to tell me it's not my fault, that it's really a joke, that it's all Chuck's fault for marrying Sandy and not letting him wear a top hat at the Pierre. I kiss each of his eyelids and he starts to growl. I look around for a second, make sure no one's watching, rest my hand on his penis and growl back.

I tell Mrs. Rinehart I want to stay at the hospital all night. Both she and my mother disagree. "I want to be here when he wakes up."

"You can come back tomorrow," Mrs. Rinehart says.

"I have to stay here," I insist. It is unthinkable that I not be here when Jake comes out of the coma. It will be four o'clock in the morning and he'll be all alone with a tube stuck in his penis and nothing to read but the Blue Cross manual. "I *have* to be here when he wakes up."

Mrs. Rinehart throws up her hands and she and my mother turn to leave. I watch their skirts disappearing down the hall. As they go around the corner, panic shoots through me and I scream. A nurse comes running into the waiting room where I sit alone with a copy of *Sports Illustrated* held up to my face. When the nurse leaves, I run down the hall in search of the mothers.

The next day I oversleep. It is one o'clock in the afternoon—practically—when I finally wake up. I notice the time and leap up from the bed, nervous with a surfeit of guilt. With my coffee, I eat a Valium and learn from the morning mail that I've been offered my

44

scholarship to attend the writers' conference. I see my-self in a crowd full of pros—Philip Roth, Robert Lowell, Nora Ephron, Joan Didion. We are having cocktails together—the five of us—slurping cocktails, nibbling hors d'oeuvres, gossiping wildly about the Mc-Govern campaign. My father's hand touches my wrist.

"I got into the conference," I say, "with a scholar-ship."

"Of course," my father says. "You win everything."

"Unless Jake isn't better," I say, "I leave next week."

"Jake is fine. He's out of the coma. Mrs. Rinehart called a few hours ago."

"She must hate me for not being there. She must think I don't even care—"

"Cut it out, woman. I'll drive you to the hospital as soon as you get dressed. You'll see Jake, he'll be fine. You'll go off to the conference, everything will work out. Okay? Do I ever lie to you?"

"It's not a question of lying, Daddy. You just can't know everything—"

"*Who* doesn't know everything?" My father's steel-blue eyes assume all determination. He is the man who knows everything. As a child, I believed him when he told me he had eyes in the back of his head. And even now, now, with the greenest, crispest, most freshly tossed of my salad days behind me, even now with Jake as finally departed as the last of all trains to Xanadu, even now I believe my father is the man who is never wrong. So odd and persistent is my belief in my father's love that I sometimes mistake his wisdom and his heart. The back of his head is ordinary: longish white curls, tanned bald skin, no special shape, no extra eye. It was his heart that could see as far as Atlantis and beyond. My father has eyes in the back of his heart.

Joan Didion hands me a cauliflowerette. I crunch on it audibly, straining to overhear the off-color joke James Dickey is whispering to Tom Wolfe. I have lost fifteen pounds and my brown hair shines blonde.

"So don't tell anybody anything, Mandy. They'll just resent you."

"Um hum," I say.

"Are you listening to me?"

"I'm listening, Daddy, but I think you're wrong. I have to at least tell Leonard. He's Jake's best friend."

"Leave it up to Jake to tell Leonard. Don't be a meddler—"

"A meddler? Jake is my—I love him as much as—I want to marry him. I'm not—"

"Just realize I know what I'm talking about."

We drive in silence for a while, but I do not summon up Joan or Wolfe or even a carrot curl.

"Daddy, do you like Jake? Still like him, I mean?"

"I love Jake," my father says.

For years those words will bring comfort. My father forgets that he ever said them, he likes Jake less after he's dead. Though most people seem to like him more.

* * *

As I walk into the hospital, I tense myself for our visit. What will I say to Jake? I should have brought a prop, a puppet—the rabbit he bought me that night in the Village when we were both sixteen. He bought me the rabbit and then I bought him the skunk. We had just seen a puppet show of *The Wizard of Oz* and he told me he'd finally decided what he wanted to be when he grew up. He wanted to be a puppet. "You mean a puppeteer?" I asked, although I knew the answer.

"No. A puppet," he said. At the time, it was the most delightful, full of delight, sweet thing a girl could hear. Jake wanted to be a puppet—fluffy, funny, something that made children laugh. Other children would have fathers who were dentists and CPAs, psychiatrists and stockbrokers, but our children would be the children of a puppet and his wife. Our children would be the children of children. Our children would be the children who made other children laugh.

What would Dr. Nold have to say about a kid who wanted to be a puppet?

I walk into intensive care and there is Jake. He is smiling enormously. I walk over to the bed. I put one hand on each of his ears. I notice there is a piece of newspaper, glued—it seems—to his forehead. It is an ad for an off-Broadway musical: *Don't Bother Me, I Can't Cope.*

I take the piece of paper off his brow and kiss the spot underneath. "You're still as funny as you used to be. But I signed permission for your lobotomy and Girlie cosigned. So if you feel kind of like a moron today . . ."

"I do feel like a moron. The psychiatrist was here, you know."

"Dr. Nold?"

"No, the hospital psychiatrist."

"What's his name?"

"Dr. Horsefeathers."

"C'mon, Jake. What did you say to the psychiatrist?"

"Nothing. I was wearing that newspaper clipping on my head."

"Did he laugh?"

"Nope."

"What did he say?"

"He asked me why I did—this—" He points around the intensive care room. To bottles and dials and screens and old women with hearts that don't beat.

"Yeah?"

"I told him I just wanted to sleep. He thinks I wanted to kill myself."

"No kidding." I make a face at him, I sneer. He looks hurt. He reaches for me. He is strong, can sit up, could do sit-ups, alive. "Yeah, no kidding, you fucking moron."

"You're mad at me," he says.

"Mad? Jake, I thought you were dead. The last twenty-four hours I spent—your mother—"

"I told my mother the same thing. I wanted to sleep."

"And what are you telling *me*?" I love this boy beyond measurement. I love him, I love him, I am him, I want him.

I look long into his face. I am him. He knows if he lies to me now, it's all over.

"I wish I was dead."

48

"Are you going to do it again?"

He doesn't answer me. I hit him in the face.

"Don't fucking hit me," he says. "I hate when you hit me."

"Goddamn you, I'll beat the shit out of you. I'm not kidding."

"If you beat me up in intensive care, they'll put you on ice for a long time, sister."

"If you're going on ice, I'm going with you. If you kill yourself, I'll kill myself. I'll die too, you fucking creep. We'll both die if you do this to me again. I'll—"

We are both crying now. He loves me. He may wish he were dead, but he loves me. His love is as thick and creamy as butter.

"Let's go to a movie," he says. "As soon as I get out of here. Let's go to a million movies in a row."

"Then you'll kill yourself when I go to buy the popcorn."

"I won't let you go. Ever."

Why is he saying this? If he won't let me go, then why is he going? If he loves me, he should want to live, but he doesn't. He loves me and he wants to be dead. I can't leave to buy popcorn, but he can check out forever.

"I feel like mangling you with my bare hands."

"I feel like mangling *your* bare hands." His voice is liquid and sexy. His voice was the first thing I loved. It will not be the last thing.

We are lying in Jake's bed the night of his release. We try to have sex, but it doesn't work. In my fantasy, we make such incredible love he wants to live and live and live, make babies and feed them, nurse at one breast while his son sucks at the other. The puppet people who kiss instead of talk and invent the world with their kisses. Me and Jake and a million babies. We never get out of bed. A million pink baby *tooshies* gleaming like polished petunias.

But we can't make it now. He can't get an erection or else he can get an erection, but it hurts me. I try to make love to him again. I kiss, kiss, kiss him.

"I still have this disgusting taste in my mouth from the coma. My tongue's all yecched out."

"I don't care. I love you. I love your body."

"I'm fat now. I'm losing my hair. I can't fuck you for more than a minute. I can't read. I can't find a job. I can't go to college. I can't make you happy. And I wish I never woke up."

"I love you, Jake."

"Well, I wish you didn't."

In the old days, a month ago, this would have been my cue to storm out. Drama was the blood, the sustenance of our relationship. And I walked out a lot and he would run after me. And he loved when I walked out so he could run after me. He would cross the highway dangerously, jumping on top of and off the divider, running recklessly across the highway, running towards me and catching me and mashing the grass with me as the drama of the chase, the false drama—there was never any doubt he would catch me—as the drama of the chase fell off into the sweet dénouement of kissing and the lovely untying of knots.

I don't walk out. I don't even get angry. I am exhausted and just want to sleep. I can't sleep here with Jake because we are only twenty years old and downstairs in the kitchen his mother is busy crying and his father is making plans for Jake's entrance into a mental hospital.

It is Annette Rinehart who calls me and asks me to come over. Jake's brother Louis is coming in from California. All the way from Los Angeles to New York. To talk to Jake. To talk about Jake. To see about admitting Jake to a hospital. Would I like to drive out to the airport with them? Would I like to have dinner with the family?

"Why didn't Jake call?"

"Mandy, he's not talking."

"Well, he'll talk to me, won't he?"

"Yes. I suppose."

"Doesn't he want me to come over?"

"I think so. I don't know, dear. But maybe once you're here, he'll come out of his room."

"Did he lock himself in?"

"Since this morning. We had a fight. His father—"

"Is he breathing?" I ask.

"Yes, Mandy. He's fine. He just won't come out of the room. Oh wait—Jake says to tell you to smuggle him in—a copy of—what, dear? Oh, Mandy, I'll call you back. He wants something."

Jake is locked in his room making smuggling jokes and Mrs. Rinehart is conveying his jokes over the telephone. His brother is flying three thousand miles to lock him up in a loony bin. Mrs. Rinehart was actually *laughing* over the telephone. Who turned out the lights?

I dress and walk over to the Rineharts' house, totally unprepared for what will happen next. In two days, my life has taken a decided turn for the worse. I smoke a joint on the way to the Rineharts'. Jake doesn't like it when I get stoned. Well, he can fuck himself. Maybe I don't like it when he eats thirty Triavils and tells the psychiatrist he feels like sleeping. I smoke pot and think about Jake's brother Louis. Louie is the psychiatrist and Chuckie is the stockbroker and Jackie is the basket case, the vegetable, the loon. Jake will make ashtrays and potholders, he will spend his twenty-first year gluing little pieces of tile to juice cans. Jake will wake up screaming. Jake will decorate his hospital room throwing his own shit against the walls.

When I get to the corner of Pennington Road, I am higher than I intended. When Annette Rinehart opens the door, I let loose a whole roomful of giggles. She smiles and doesn't find me peculiar. Why is she so cheerful?

"Jake still has the door locked, but he's been fooling around. I'm sure he'll open the door for you."

"When is Louis coming?"

"Around dinnertime."

"Is Louis going to have him committed to a hospital?"

"We'll see."

"Let me in, Jack."

"Who is it?"

"It's Dr. Horsefeathers."

"Do you know what they're planning to do to me?"

"It's not settled yet."

"Well, I'm not fucking going into any mental hospital. I'm not crazy. My own mother thinks I'm crazy."

"Let me in, Jake."

"No, I'm not opening this door till they promise they won't put me in a hospital. Do you think I'm crazy, Mandy?"

"Yes, Jake. Now let me in."

"Do you really think I'm crazy?"

"I think you're crazy to make me stand here in the hall."

"Who's *making* you do anything?"

"Jake, let me in. Don't lock me out, baby. Please don't lock me out."

Louis is almost as short as Jake. His eyes are blue, like their mother's. Louis is cuter than Chuck, but neither of them is really handsome. Jake is the handsomest. Jake looks like Paul McCartney.

I have met Louis only twice before. When he got engaged to Andrea and they both flew out here. That was three years ago. And at Jake's grandfather's funeral. That was mere months ago. I can't tell if Louis likes me or not. I think he thinks I should invest in a good brassiere. I think he thinks I'm some hippie chick with a fish between my legs.

We are sitting in a Chinese restaurant. I have a headache and so does Louis. We compare our headaches. Mine is sharp and it feels, I tell him, like someone is scraping my brain with a shovel.

"Why a shovel?" Jake asks.

"I don't know. That's the image."

"Why a shovel?" Jake asks again.

No one talks for a long time. Louis slumps down for a second and soon he is fast asleep, his head resting lightly in a plateful of soy-stained rice. "Jet lag," Manny Rinehart says, reaching into his pocket for his Bank Americard. "Jet lag," he says as Annette Rinehart rouses her oldest son.

In the parking lot, Jake puts his arms around me. "Why a shovel?" he says.

When we get back to the house, Annette Rinehart points out the Cadillac taking up their driveway. Louis looks at the car and moans. "Who is it?" I nudge Jake.

"It's the *machetaynestes*," he says.

54

"The what?"

"Tell her, Ma."

"The in-laws, he means. The Greenwalds."

So nobody likes the Greenwalds. I am part of a family conspiracy. I am practically Jake's wife already. My mother and father are practically *machetaynestes* themselves.

Mimi Greenwald is wearing a mink Eisenhower jacket in August. She is a still-pretty woman, but when she gives Jake her cheek to kiss, his face comes up orange. Jake makes believe he has to tell me a secret. When I bend in towards his mouth to hear it, he wipes his makeup-stained cheek on my nose. "Why a shovel?" he says.

Annette Rinehart doesn't pretend she is happy to see them. Mimi is hardly out of her mink when she asks Annette, "So what's wrong?"

"Everything's fine," Annette says. "So you want cream in your coffee?"

Mimi points to her watch, then taps it. One carved russet fingernail taps on Tiffany. "It's after six. No coffee for me after six."

"So tell me, Annette, what's wrong?" I am in the women's corner. Louis and Jake have disappeared into the family room. Manny and Ben Greenwald sit in the opposite corner. Manny is holding a bottle of Scotch. He is swirling the liquid in the bottle. Both men watch as the gold liquid washes around the glass.

"Nothing is wrong, Mimi."

"If nothing's wrong, why is Louis here? Why is he

here without Andrea? Have they moved Los Angeles to across the street?"

"I'll get your coffee."

Mimi Greenwald looks at me as if I am the family dog, or an interesting piece of cloth. Her hand strokes my head and one fingernail gets hooked by a knot in my hair. Mimi Greenwald extricates her finger from my head.

"So what's new?" she says.

"I met you at Louis's engagement party—and then at the funeral."

"Of course, dear. You're Jackie's little friend."

"I'm Mandy Charney," I say.

Annette comes back with cups of coffee.

"No coffee for me after six," Mimi Greenwald says. She sighs, exhaling deeply. Annette Rinehart's ordinarily pretty face has taken on the determined set of a bulldog's. Mimi Greenwald will get no info out of her. She could rake those stiletto fingernails across Annette's face from now till six o'clock tomorrow. She could, in a special matron's version of the old Oriental rite, drip tiny drop upon tiny drop of Chanel No. 5 down Annette's face. Annette would tell her nothing. She will protect her children from this mink-coated commando, and from anyone else who dares invade the privacy of her children's psyches. Sitting there on the velvet love-seat, four feet eleven in her peds, she is the littlest, bravest, most impenetrable of prisoners of war. Mimi Greenwald is a bad guy. Annette Rinehart is a good guy. Our white hats flapping elegantly behind us, we

will gallop into any sunset, Jake's secret heart our
bounty and reward.

Manny and Ben are laughing. They are drinking
shots of whiskey and telling stories. "Mimi!" Ben roars
from across the room. "What was the name of that guy
—that dentist?"

"I don't remember," Mimi says, flatly, disconsolately.
Of course she remembers the name of the dentist, there
is nothing that woman doesn't remember. Including the
smallish hole in the sweater I wore to the grandfather's
funeral. (When she sees that hole for the second time, a
very few months from now, at another, sadder, funeral,
she will remember to include me out from all social
occasions which demand that the celebrants wear
black.)

Mimi drinks not one, but two cups of coffee before
she gets up to retrieve her husband from the other love-
seat. "Come, Ben," she says, "we have to be going.
Where are the children?" I follow her into the den, just
in case, where Jake and Louis are watching a rerun of
The Honeymooners. So Louis has flown three thousand
miles to watch Jackie Gleason three hours earlier. Mimi
and I are thinking exactly the same incriminating
thought.

"Vultures," Annette Rinehart says, closing the door.
"He's a nice guy," Manny says, perhaps feeling

slightly foolish that he and Mr. Vulture have gotten along so well.

Louis drives me home. We sit in the car for a few minutes.

"Are you going to commit him?"

"I'm not going to commit him. I will suggest that he go into a hospital, but I can't very well commit my own brother."

"Of course not," I whisper, relieved. "Do you—did you get to talk to him?"

"Sort of," Louis says. "But we're brothers, you know. We, um—listen, Mandy, it's up to him. He may want to die, but he wants to live, too. He does, he has to. He was always a pretty funny person—even as a kid."

"But funny doesn't mean happy," I say.

"No, it doesn't. I'm not sure if you realize how hard this is for me." In the rearview mirror I allow myself a look into his fishy, cold blue eyes. They are sad eyes now, wet eyes. Now they don't look fishy. They are the eyes of a man whose brother's life has just been handed to him.

"I know this sounds silly, unprofessional for a doctor. But Jake can't want to die. We love him too much."

"It doesn't sound silly," I say. We are both crying now and we sit there crying. Between us there is no stick shift or other encumbrance, and yet we do not hug. It remains peculiar to me, now in the car, and later, after Jake's gone, how difficult it becomes to hug any man without a fear of sex. Death, I am learning, introduces

58

its own aesthetic. And death and eroticism seem sweaty cousins, clammy but familiar old friends.

"Everybody loves everybody too much," Jake says. We are sitting in the park next to the petting zoo. "And it doesn't do anybody a bit of good. Everyone is miserable anyway."

"I'm not miserable."

"Sure, you're not miserable. I *know* what I'm doing to you. I know what I'm doing to my mother. Today she was reading the comics at breakfast. The *comics*," Jake says.

"So?"

"My mother doesn't *read* comics."

"What are you saying, Jake? So your mother read the comics. Big deal."

"She's acting weird. And so are you. Every time I leave the house, she looks at me like it's—"

"Well, what do you expect? It could be."

"I won't do it," he says.

"Do you mean it?"

"I won't kill myself on one condition."

"What?"

"You take off all your clothes and get in there with the piglets."

Off to the right is a pen full of piglets. They are as soft and preformed as a fleet of fontanels.

"You're an idiot," I say.

"You're a piglet. Take off your panties and get in there."

"Jake, it isn't funny. I have to know if you're going to do it."

"Well, what will you do if I say I might?"

"I'll never let you out of my sight. I'll follow you to the bathroom. I'll pay you a dollar a day in bribes."

"You *owe* me forty dollars."

"I'm not paying you back."

"Forty dollars is forty days."

"You're horrible," I say. "How can you sit here and make this into a joke—?"

"It's *my* fucking life, Mandy. If I choose to think it's funny, it's funny. So quit hassling me."

"*Hassling* you, do you have any idea—?"

"Look, I said I know what I'm doing to you. But the more I do it, the more I hate myself. And the more I hate myself, the more I want to—"

"No!" I say. "No."

In the distance, a piglet squeals. In the distance a child screams, "Fuck Mommy!" In the distance, over the lake where small boys sail smaller ships, my childhood yawns and collapses.

Jake puts a hand on my breast. He kisses my ear. He touches my neck. There in the petting zoo we kiss as wetly and hotly as if alone in the world.

"Kiss me," I say. "Kiss me." Even as I am being kissed, "kiss me," I say.

Before Louis leaves for Los Angeles, he and Jake make a deal. Louis knows a doctor in Boston. Louis and Andrea are flying to Boston in a week or so for some doctors' conference. Louis will be reading a paper. Jake promises to fly up to Boston and check the hospital out.

"It's a hippie hospital," Jake says. "You come and go and stuff. I *hate* the idea of a hippie hospital more than a regular loony bin."

"But it's good to be able to come and go."

"But I'll have to sit in encounter groups. Have you ever *been* to one of those things?"

"Have you?" I ask.

"Yeah. Dr. Nold had me in one of those groups. It's really depressing. These fat girls with pimples crying . . ."

"Not all hippies have pimples."

"The ones in these groups do."

"Well, you have to at least try it."

"I'll go up there. In a week or so. But I don't want to be away from you. . . ."

"But I have to leave. . . ."

"Not till September. Right?"

"Well, there's this writers' conference. I won a scholarship."

"You did? Why didn't you tell me?"

"I just found out the day you got out of the hospital."

"Well you can still *tell* me things. Can't you? Goddammit, Mandy, why don't you tell me things?"

"I do tell you. I'm telling you now. I *want* to go to it."

"For how long?"

"A week."

"Where?"

"New Hampshire."

"When?"

"It starts in a week."

He looks at me sadly. He pouts.

"There'll be famous people there."

"As famous as me?"

"No," I say. "No one's as famous as you."

"I *am* famous," he says. "I *was* on *The Joe Franklin Show.*"

"You'll be even *more* famous if you decide to stick around for a while."

"Forty days," he says. "Do you suppose in the next forty days me and Leonard could get discovered?"

"You don't mean this forty days stuff, do you, Jake?"

"Sure I do. At least until you pay me back."

"I think you're a famous moron," I say. "A famous sadist. A famous asshole."

"Flaming asshole, you mean."

The next week passes in this same strange mood of double-talk and double meaning. Half the time, when we forget about it, when I forget about it, we behave like any twenty-year-olds who are deeply, obscurely, darkly in love. We kiss and watch movies. We kiss and read each other stories. We kiss and talk and make exuberant love to each other's bodies. But always there is the shadow of something kinetic, of something alive. It is almost a presence, this imminence of death. Jake has one flat foot in the grave. He knows it. I know it. Annette and Manny know it. Louis knows it, and he's a doctor. Even Mimi Greenwald can feel, through the fatty layers of her suspicious heart, some presentiment of loss.

I know that Jake is miserable, but I leave him anyway to go off to the writers' conference. It is not only that I want to rub parts with luminaries. It is not only that I want to hear what the experts have to say about my stories, my articles, my sad villanelles. I want to get away from the faraway scent of death. I want to get away from the talk of mental hospitals. I want to get away from Jake.

Preparing to leave him, I begin to welcome guilts of all names into my psyche. Guilt takes over all my emotions. Guilt is the fat lady who crowds all the other guests out of the rooming house. Guilt is the slob who sweats and sobs and fans herself lazily with a three-color advertisement for trusses and sickroom aids. Guilt is the smell of the fat woman's feet, her squat, corn-plastered toes tortured into wedgies; the smell of her tiredness the same good-bad smell as that of burned lasagna, reheated for this, the fourth and final time.

At the bus station, Jake is anxious.

"I know you don't want me to go."

"I do. I want you to be happy."

"*You* make me happy," I say, lying. My voice is as thin as newsprint.

Jake has that look in his cow-brown eyes. It is, I assure myself, the medication, the antidepressants that make him look so obsessed, like an animal in dread pursuit. His pupils are nearly as large as the brown parts of his eyes. Behind his smile is neither humor nor joy. Behind his smile is the chemical diagram for Triavil.

"While you're gone," he says, "I may go up to Boston. I may go up and see that doctor."

"If you go up to Boston, you'll be practically in New

Hampshire. You can come up to New Hampshire. We can sleep together."

"I may go into the hospital, you know."

"I thought you were dead set against it." Nervously I consider the awkwardness of my pun.

"I don't know, Mandy. What do you think?"

"If you go into the hospital, you'll have to dance with the old ladies."

Jake looks at me. Only a year ago, when Jake was in college in Vermont, he worked at a mental hospital. Only a year ago, Jake was on the right side of the key. He dropped out of that college, an experimental hippie campus, after three months—a record of endurance. But even after he'd dropped out, he'd continued to go off to the state institution where he played his washboard and spoons, and sometimes danced with the old ladies. Now he will be one of them. An inmate. A loon. A basket case. Crazy. Cuckoo. Not all there. Already he is not all there. Part of him is dead. Part of him is made out of Triavil.

I have said the wrong thing. Jake says nothing, but with that simple sentence I have said too much.

"You'll have to dance with the old ladies." That sentence reveals all my bitterness, that sentence speaks all my contempt. Later, much later, when I am grown up, when I am grown and married to somebody else, when I am grown and nourishing someone else's baby with the blood and the milk and the kisses that were intended for Jake's own son, later that line will reawaken every time, every time I hear it, thinly, in my mind's ear, the failure I will carry throughout my life—my failure to have made the difference between his life and his death.

* * *

"I'm sorry," I say.

"For what?"

"I'm just sorry."

"Well, quit being sorry."

"I didn't mean it—about the old ladies."

"What about the old ladies?"

"I didn't mean it," I say.

As the bus pulls out of the station, I see him for what could be the last time. He is small, just five five, and he looks young for twenty. His hair is receding from his forehead. At twenty he has not enough hair to really resemble Paul McCartney. It is nine years, I realize, since he introduced himself to the drama group as Lightbeam, nine years since I first loved that pretty face, that funny, funny mouth. Out of that mouth came the funniest words I would ever hear. Out of that mouth came the sweetest kisses I would ever swallow. I know, even at twenty, I know as the bus pulls out of Forty-first Street and over to Tenth Avenue, I know that Jake was sent into the world to love me and give me babies. I know, contradictorily, that it is already too late.

II

U<small>P IN</small> N<small>EW</small> H<small>AMPSHIRE</small> the luminaries sit at their own table, hang out at their own cottage, drink their own liquor, exchange their own bons mots. My fantasies of camaraderie and passionate gossip with big shots never come true.

The first night I am befriended by a thirty-year-old woman of the world. What makes her a woman of the world in my eyes is the fact that she is the mistress of a well-known man, the executive editor of an important literary semimonthly. That she sleeps with him is the first thing she tells me.

"Hi," she says, shaking my hand, shaking her body, shaking everything, "I'm Bitsy Mosel." And then in a lower voice: "And I'm here because I'm Ezra Winer's mistress."

When I say nothing, she nudges me hard. "Don't you even know who he is?"

69

"Of course I do," I say.

"Well, Ez has been encouraging me to write this thing—it's kind of an exposé of Fellini. You know who Fellini is, don't you, baby?"

"Um hum. Do you know him? Personally, I mean?"

"Oh, yes. He practically invented me. You see I was in *Satyricon*. Did you see *Satyricon*, baby?"

"No. You're an actress?"

"Umm. No. Yes. A little. I've been on television and stuff, but acting isn't even fun. They practically torture you to death. Federico glued my eyes shut for one scene —the scene when the—"

"I didn't see—"

"Of course not, baby. Anyway, I'm much more of a writer than an actress. I love to write. Don't you just love it?"

"More like a flirtation."

"A flirtation! How marvelous! You're incredibly clever, aren't you? We'll be best friends and I'll teach you everything. How to put on makeup, clothes, everything. You wouldn't believe how many clothes I brought up here—"

Bitsy squints across the long room, an old converted barn. "So *there's* Donald Dempson," she says. "Aren't you absolutely mad for that old man?"

"I've never met him," I say.

"Do you have affairs?" She winks.

"What do you mean? With married men?"

"No, affairs, plain affairs. With anybody."

"Do I sleep with people, you mean?"

"Yeah. That's what I mean."

"I sleep with my boyfriend."

"Well, Donald's married to this absolutely masochistic little girl named Pamela, but of course he would never *dream* of bringing her. . . ."

"Listen, Bitsy, I'm not quite old enough for him, don't you think?"

"Of course not, baby, you're only sixteen, aren't you? How about if I see you later? I'll come up to your room and tell you bedtime stories. . . . Like the time I was thrown out of the Saint—Ooh, I'm starting to wet my pants. . . ."

Bitsy is easily the hit of the conference. She is not the most intelligent woman there, nor is she even the prettiest. But there is something about her that draws all the eligible and ineligible men to her door. She has a kind of vulgar charm that all the uptight literary types seem to find irresistible. Probably their wives are Ph.D.s with pieces of spinach caught in their teeth. Bitsy is like a little girl—all talk and showing off, very little action. It takes Billy Reese six whole days to get inside her Pucci panties. Or so Bitsy reassures me.

Part of my attraction to Bitsy is the sense that she is not real. I suppose she has in her life experienced one sort or another of pain, but it is hard to believe. She is my opposite—a napper till noon, a sybarite, a believer in the power of good wines and vitamin C.

A boy flirts with me at dinner. We are eating stewed tomatoes and Swiss steak and Jell-O cubes.

"What kinda stuff you write?" he asks.

71

"Lately, kind of experimental stuff. Really short things?"

"You mean like minimal fiction?"

"Kind of. I'm trying to play with the idea of time. . . ."

"Oh yeah?" he says. His teeth are enormous. He has the look of a very healthy horse. "Oh yeah?" he says, smiling. His shoulders are large, his legs are muscular, his hair is as thick as ropes.

He walks me to the Stable, the large converted barn, the hangout. We sidle against the wall and make small talk. The couple next to us are dressed alike in *New York* magazine tee shirts. The woman punches the man in the arm. The man punches the woman.

"Look," the Horsey Boy says. "I dig you."

I laugh nervously.

"You want to come to my room and ball?"

"No," I say. Do I?

"You want me to go away, then?"

"If you want."

He shakes his head appraisingly.

"I dig you," he says.

"In New York," I say, "I have a boyfriend. He's in . . . really bad shape."

"Is he strung out?"

"He's mentally ill."

"Far out," the Horsey Boy says. "A schizo. Is that what you like—schizos?" His laugh is throaty and cruel, the sexual edge like razor blades floating in a tub of ice. "I'm a reporter, you know."

"For who?"

"I, like, have my own magazine."

"Where?"

"Chicago. I own the whole fucking magazine. I'm a goddamn hippie fascist. But I just do reporting and let this woman be the publisher."

"That's nice of you."

"Look, I'm not nice at all. I'm a pig. But maybe you like pigs."

"I'm not sure. They say every woman adores a fascist."

"That's really true," he says. He looks happy.

"I didn't make that up."

"Listen, your name is—"

"Mandy . . . Mandy Charney."

"I'm Dover," he says. "Dover Fielding."

"Are you a preppie?" I ask.

"I think I went to Exeter in a former life."

"I don't like preppies," I say.

"Of course not. You're into schizos."

"I like basket cases."

"Sure. I bet you *really* go for guys who can't get it up."

"I love them."

"I bet you like to be fucked so hard your guts spill onto the sheets."

"Yes," I say. "How'd you guess?"

"I bet you . . ." All of a sudden I am crying. Dover looks at me with disbelief. "I'm sorry." His voice is soft as puppies. "I'm sorry, Mandy. I was freaking on you."

"It's not you," I say. "I like you."

"You wanna ball *now*?" he says.

"That's not it."

"You want me to hug you?" he asks. He hugs me then, tight and hard. I melt into his chest. His sweater is

Mexican wool and heavy and gives off the scent of heady grass.

"We can go somewhere and talk," he says.

"Okay, but no sex. Okay?"

"No sex whatsoever," he says. "None. Zero. Zilch."

Dover's roommate is a small child of maybe eleven or twelve. His mother is a member of the teaching faculty, a semi-important structuralist. His father died mysteriously while campaigning for office in a California border town. Or so go the rumors.

Fish is sitting on the dresser swinging his legs when we walk in. He is singing "Norwegian Wood" along with the radio. He is smoking one joint and holding a backup.

"Dover," says Fish. "This is good crap."

"Good *shit*, Fish. Not crap."

"Yeah, well it's good crap. Did you see my mom?"

"She was humping this large-breasted woman. . . ."

"Yeah," Fish says. It is unclear whether he believes Dover or not. "You want to ball?" he asks. I laugh. "No," he says. "Not with me. I thought maybe I should leave—in case you two wanted to ball."

"The expression is orb," Dover says, "not ball."

"Yeah, orb," Fish says. "Okay. You folks want to *orb* or can I plan to hang around?"

"I don't want to orb anybody."

"Me neither," Dover says.

"I wouldn't mind an orb or two," Fish says solemnly. "There *is* a chick my age here. The director's daughter."

"Well go to her room and nail her," Dover says.

"Yeah. I was kinda thinking about it."

"What's your real name?" I ask him.

"Mine?" He has finished one joint and has lit the second.

"Fish is my last name. My first name is Eric."

"Can I call you Eric?" I ask.

"Call me whatever you want."

"Let's go down to the creek," Dover says. "We can throw stones against the rocks."

At the creek, we sit down on cold boulders. The air is wet with distillation, evaporation, mist. The sky has a look of blue under black. It looks like the dark velvet lining of an angel's overcoat. The stars are stud pins, buttons, the stars are not real tonight.

"*I* know," Eric says. "Let's all tell what we think love means."

"You first," Dover says.

"Me?" Eric says. "Uh-uh."

"Do you love anybody special?" I ask him.

"I loved my father a lot. But it's easy to love people who are dead."

"You're right," I say.

"You don't have to be good to them. You don't have to remember their favorite ice cream flavor."

"You're getting carried away," Dover says. "You're such a fucking clever little fart."

"You *are* incredibly wise for your age." I touch Eric's head.

"Yeah. If I really *was* smart I'd fuck my mother and get it over with."

"Why don't you?"

"Don't listen to Dover," I say. "He has no idea what he's saying."

"My mother wouldn't fuck me," Eric says. "I'd have to fucking rape her."

"Your mother would love it," Dover says. "She'd love it to pieces. Goddamn!"

Eric looks at me imploringly. "My mom's a dyke," he says.

"I didn't know that."

"Yeah, well, it's weird."

"I'm sure."

"My boyfriend just tried to kill himself." I am trying to make Eric feel less lonely. I am trying to let him know he's not the only person alive.

"How'd he do it?" Eric asks.

"Pills," I say.

"Then he doesn't want to die," Dover says. "If he really wanted to die, he'd shoot himself. In the mouth. Like this—" Dover opens his mouth. He forms a gun with his hairy left hand and pretends to shoot himself.

"I think he does want to die," I say. "Only no one will believe him. I believe him, but I can't stand it. I can't stand to even *be* with him."

I am astonished by the sound of my words. The words come out of my mouth, but beyond that, they are not

mine. The words fly out of my mouth like large, independent, white-winged birds, birds of incredible wing
span. They fly out of my mouth and into the universe.
They roost on a telephone wire and caw.

"When I was seven," Eric says, "I walked in on my
parents. My mom was wearing a black slip. She was tied
to the bed with ties. One of the ties musta broke off,
'cause always after that I remember a piece of the tie on
the bedpost. My father's red-and-blue striped tie. I
think he bought it in Princeton when he was a drama—"

In the misty silver light of the universe, Eric is slop-
pily crying. He blows his nose, hard, in the air. His face
is streaked with mucus and tears.

I reach over for him. I hold him. He smells like
Maypo and Bosco, like liquid Joy and yellow mustard.
American, adolescent, alive.

"Eric," I say. "You're a wonderful boy. I love you," I
say.

"I love you, too, man," Dover says. "And it's groovy
the way you remember that stuff. That piece of the tie
on the bedpost. You'll be a great writer for sure. You're
like some little Proust. You'll shame the rest of us out
of the business. In a few years women like Bianca Jagger
will be mailing you their dirty panties."

I start to laugh and Eric starts to laugh. Dover is
wonderful, too. We all three are in love.

In the morning, everyone makes a big fuss over the
mail. We have only been up here on the mountain for

three days, but everyone is extremely anxious for communication with the outside. Everyone, perhaps, but me. I would be happy to stay on the mountain forever. On the mountain with Bitsy and Eric and Dover. Everything sounds funny up here on the mountain, up here, away from the world. In my mailbox there are two letters from Jake.

DEAR MANDY,

I wrote this while you were still in N.Y. In fact, I wrote this while you were lounging on my bed. Girlie says "hi." I would say "hi" too, but I can't because I have a large turtle sitting in my mouth and all communication is difficult.

I was in N.H. once when I was nine years old. My parents rented a cabin and me and Chuck and Louis all slept in one bed. It was fun.

Love,
JAKE

I read his letter twice and my sinuses start to burn. Do people really die from broken hearts? All those stories of women dying of cancer, their husbands sniffing at their graves so longingly they fall in after. And Elaine, the Lily Maid of Astolat, her pale virgin's body parting finally for the river alone. Lancelot let her die—his heart was too pure for love. But what about Guinevere? For Guinevere, he was impure plenty.

Don't make us die, Jake, because the world is not pure. Two teenagers dead in a car across the river in New Jersey. Protesting the war in Vietnam, they turn on the carbon monoxide and cuddle, the voice of Murray the K lulling them to sleep forever. Moved by the sorrows of young Werther, hundreds of German youths suicide in tribute to romantic love. And time takes the nieces and nephews of these lost German children and makes them into the administrators of death camps and factories. Of laboratories where the strength of the human heart is put to tests more brutal than the Angel of Death himself could imagine. Theories reach us in America that it was the bad Jews who survived, but every single human being knows this is not true. In the cattle cars, on the way to Dachau, corpses were discovered in the act of making love.

I am sleeping that night in a narrow cot when I am awakened by the feeling of blood, the smell of blood, its terror and taste. I wake up to find I'm not dreaming. The blood is literal, red and warm. The sheets, my nightgown, the coverlet, are wet with red-black blood.

I take myself into the bathroom and began washing everything. The blood, now pinkish and muted, swirls endlessly into the sink. Bitsy Mosel comes in from a date.

"Baby!" she screams.

Her hair is knotted and matted. Her skin is greenish in the fluorescent light.

"You look terrible," I say. It is I who am standing naked washing blood from bedclothes.

"What happened?" she asks.

"I think I was hemorrhaging."

"What are you going to do?"

"Let's just get some sleep."

"I saw that terrible little boy again," Bitsy says.

"You mean Fish?"

"Um hum. He sure is a strange one," she says. "He asked where you were."

"Did you tell him I was sleeping?"

"I told him to find someone his own age. To pick on, I think I said."

"He's a special person," I say.

"His mother is a lesbian."

"Lots of people are lesbians."

"I'm not," Bitsy says. "Are you?"

"No, Bitsy," I say.

When I wake up, I am bleeding rather conventionally again. Never do I discover what caused me to lose all that blood. I am a different person these days. I have given up on the idea of cause and effect. The blood was some sort of ritual sacrifice to everyone who wants to see Jake dead. The blood was spilled for the vultures. My miscarriage, if that's what it was, was merely my body's vain effort to reproduce Jake's twin.

Eric is sitting on my cot when I get back from my eleven o'clock seminar on Neo-New Criticism.

"Mandy," he says, "I don't know why I'm here."

"Don't you?" I ask.

"I think I don't want to fuck you."

"Why not?"

"Because—I'm an idiot."

"Did you go backpacking this morning?"

"I walked around for a while with no pack."

"Should we go to lunch?" I ask.

"No. It's ravioli tetrazzini parmigiana. It sucks," he says.

"Eric," I say. But it's no use. He is crying now, his tiny hands pushing my pillow into his puckered face.

His face is ordinary, or maybe it is ugly. His nose is too big for his face. Tiny bloodspots of dried acne, a few softish yellow beard hairs—nothing functional enough to call stubble.

I kiss, on purpose I kiss, one scarred acne-spot. "Eric," I say.

"I'm sorry," he says.

"Don't be so sorry." I am speaking Jake's words. Whenever I tell Jake I'm sorry, he says, "Don't be *so* sorry." It is that tiny word "so" that always works, that always makes me feel less sorry. "Don't be so sorry, Eric."

"I *hate* New Hampshire. If we were in New York, we could sit at the Fountain."

"And what would we do at the Fountain?"

"There's hippies, everywhere."

"We could count hippies." Eric laughs at my joke.

"We could buy loose joints and smoke them," he says.

"Eric, you're plenty loose already. If you want some pot, I'll steal some from Bitsy. She has great pot that Billy Reese gave her."

"Billy Reese is a moron."

"Why does everyone hate him?" I ask.

"Because he has horrible vibes. If he breathes on you, it fucks up your karma. For a week."

"Is your mother sleeping with him?"

"My mom is a dyke, Mandy. Why does everyone never believe me?"

"I believe you, Eric. But these things—sex—are never absolute."

"Absolute," he says.

"You sit here with the pillow and I'll go find you some pot."

Bitsy's pot is like magic. As golden as Labradors, it is magic and good. We sniff, smoke, snort, sniff it. Eric's face looks like the moon, his acne-pits are craters. One large C-shaped scar, seashaped, curls into itself and giggles. In the middle of this gory red sea, I see love. It is scary love, scurvy love, there are ghosts in it. It is a bloody, bloodstained love. It is lovelessness come true.

Do I have to kiss every leper in the world in order to be holy? Or can I just kiss some, a couple, two, three lepers? My father thinks I should kiss no lepers at all. Jake kisses all the lepers—but secretly. He wears his love like a sin, like a stain. Is Eric my Thin Girl Afraid of Everything? If I love Eric will Jake then not die?

Eric's lips are brutal. He kisses me, close-mouthed, with his teeth. His hard teeth bump my soft chin. His teeth knock at my mouth like bones.

"Lemme in, lemme in," speaks his sad tongue, but I prefer to kiss him this way. "Lemme, lemme in," speaks dark, sweet Eric. Dark-souled, brooding, as young as thirteen new brides.

"Eric, Eric, I do really love you."

"Mmm," he says as he nuzzles my chest. He places

one hand on each of my breasts. My breasts are like nations, each one a mother.

He is down on the bed now and I am on top. His pelvis is dream-miles away from my pelvis, but Bitsy Mosel understands and believes in only what she can see.

"Bab—" Oh. Uh-oh. Uh-oh.

"It's okay, Bitsy."

"Well, you two—what *are* you two doing? Baby, are you crazy?"

"I'm crazy about Eric. He's crazy about me. We are *not* screwing, we are cuddling, and quit hassling me."

Eric lights the reefer.

"Lighten up, Bitsy."

Eric and I don't make love.

"Who's paying for this?" Jake and I have been on the phone for forty-five minutes easy.

"Dorothy Kilgallen," he says. She is our code word for fake credit cards.

"Well, even so," I say. "We still better get off."

"You wanna hear what I did in the act last night? I said to this man, 'Hey mister, your cigarette is on fire.' Nobody laughed. Well, there was this one retarded guy who laughed at everything I said. Retarded people understand me."

"I'm a retard," I say. "I understand you."

"You only wrote me two letters and I wrote you six."

"I'll be home soon."

"Come home early."

"But you're going to Boston anyway."

"I'll wait for you and we'll both go to Boston."

"How long will Louis be there?"

"Till Thursday night."

"The conference doesn't end till Friday."

"*Please* come home early."

"I paid eighty dollars for a personal conference. I can't just blow it off."

"Blow *me* off instead."

"Please, Jake, I *have* to. I *have* to. Go to Boston and I'll meet you there Friday night. Maybe Louis and Andrea have friends who'll let us sleep together."

"No one will let us sleep together."

"Yes they will. It'll be okay."

"Mandy, I need you. I've been driving around past your house every night. I need you *with* me."

"I have to go now, Jake. I'll call you tomorrow on Dorothy K."

"I love you Mandy," he whimpers.

"I love *you you you*," I say, hanging up the phone. "You."

Billy Reese wants to take Bitsy to lunch. Bitsy insists that if he wants to take her, he has to take her friends. So Dover and Fish and I get taken out to lunch. Billy Reese spends seventy dollars wooing Bitsy, who only eats the cheese off the open-face crab-and-cheese sandwich she orders after first making sure the crab is Dungeness.

"Yummy," Bitsy says.

"Why dontcha eat a little more of that fancy sandwich?" Billy says.

"This crab is *not* Dungeness," Bitsy says. "I *know*

what a Dungeness crab is. I was practically raised on them."

"In the Midwest?" Dover says. "You were raised on crab in the Midwest?"

"Yes," Bitsy says. "I had a very expensive childhood."

Dover and Eric start pushing their elbows into each other's sides. Pushing their elbows and laughing. Dover jabs Fish in the waist sharply and this time a decanter of wine gets toppled. A Petit Sirah from the Mondavi Vineyards seeps into Bitsy's expensive white shirt.

"Damn you all!" Bitsy says hysterically. "I try to do something *nice* for you and this is how you repay me." Bitsy is crying openly now. She pushes her plate away from her and asks for a cigarette.

"But you don't even smoke," I say.

"I'm starting right now. I'm going to smoke Chesterfields. Millions of them."

"*You* got the lady upset," Billy says. "*You* got her upset and I'm gonna have to *do* something about it." Billy picks Eric up by the shirt collar.

"Not him," I say. "He's thirteen years old."

"And I'm very expensive," Eric giggles.

Billy hits Eric squarely against the nose. When the blood comes, it is orangish, it is a sickly red-orange color, and it causes me to gag. Bitsy is not gagging. She is staring in open-eyed delight.

"Listen, Reese," Dover says. "If I try to hit you, you'll beat the shit outta me. Right?"

Billy snarls.

"I mean willya? 'Cause if you won't hit me back, I'll hit you. Okay? Hard. But you gotta promise you won't hit me back."

Billy starts laughing and so does Dover. Billy shoves

Dover playfully, picks up the decanter, spills the last dribble of Petit Sirah onto the tablecloth. When that decanter is empty, Billy lifts the other decanter and begins to empty that one.

"Billy!" Bitsy coos. "Billy! Pour me a little bit first." Bitsy is having the time of her life.

Billy pours the rest of the wine down the back of Bitsy's expensive white shirt. The wine is expensive, too. Nine dollars a liter for domestic Petit Sirah. Bitsy is crying again. Her hair is matted with wine. Her eye makeup blackens the sides of her nose.

"It's all your fault!" she tells Eric, who is drumming on the tabletop with one hand, holding his damaged nose with the other. "It's all your fault for ruining a lovely lunch!"

"Don't blame the kid," Billy says. "C'mon kid, have a drink. On me."

"Sure," Eric says. "Cutty Sark."

"Cutty Sark," Dover says. And then he starts laughing uncontrollably.

"Waituh," Billy says. "Waituh!"

The waiter is a smallish androgynous man of maybe twenty-five.

"I can't serve Scotch to a minor. I *know* he had some of that wine. And besides you people are behaving terribly. There is wine all over everything."

"Waituh, I said I *need* a bottle, hear me, a bottle of Cutty Sark at this table. Right here. Give me a bottle of Cutty Sark and a glass here for my friend."

"I will do no such thing. You people are *bleeding* all over the restaurant. I'm going to have to ask you to leave."

"Listen, waituh. Yuh got ten seconds to bring me a bottle of Cutty Sark. Ten seconds. Eric, start counting."

Dully, Eric starts counting. "One Mississippi, two Mississippi . . ."

"Mississippi!" Billy hollers. "I love, love, love it! You're awright, Eric. Keep on counting."

The waiter swoops to remove the wineglasses from the table. He bends over Billy's place, his fingers now encircling the stem of Billy's glass. Billy's hand comes down on the waiter's hand, two hands locked, locked in a witless battle over an empty glass. Billy's hand tightens. The waiter's weaker hand stupidly does not relent. The stem snaps off then, and every one of us looks on in horror as the waiter's white palm spits blood.

Bitsy lets out a wail. A deeply hysterical and psychotic sound.

"My God," the waiter says, "my God."

I take the waiter's hand in my hand. I hold it as I would a child's hand. We are crossing some enormous and momentous boulevard. All the lights are against us. The blood is all over both of us now, our hands clenched in a ruddy knot.

It is this moment that Billy chooses to upend the table. With one heave of his bully's body, Bitsy's lovely luncheon is spent. Under the table there moves a river of water and blood and wine. Carried away in this river are tips of asparagus, fragments of glass, the bruised flesh of the sinewy crab.

Eric's nose starts bleeding again in the back seat of Billy's jeep. I sit next to Eric, harboring his small frame against me. In the front seat, Bitsy is giggling at something Dover has said. We are going back to the conference to see if the director can't use his influence in securing Billy's release from jail.

In the morning of the next day, Billy recounts his story at a breakfast of scrapple and porridge. Bitsy is giggling and smiling. Billy is such a bad old boy, such a good-bad boy, such a fun-loving rascal. And I am sick to my stomach. The scrapple resembles nothing I have ever considered food. I move away from these people, my friends. I move away from Bitsy and Billy and search the room for Eric. I see his mother at the luminaries' table and brace myself for the approach. She is a good-looking, even great-looking woman, with enormous brown eyes and thick, streaked hair. Perhaps Eric will also grow beautiful some day. But the possibility seems as remote as the idea that the mother will someday let the son make love to her.

"Ms. Farcas," I say, feeling ridiculous pronouncing the "mizz."

"Sondra," she says.

"Sondra, I'm Mandy Charney—a friend of Eric's," I say.

"Fish pointed you out." How odd that a mother—any mother—could call her son by his father's last name. I wonder what she called his father.

"Well, how's his nose doing?"

"It's broken," she says. "Reese is a complete asshole,

but I'm willing to let the whole thing drop if Coggins promises not to rehire him."

. I am shocked and delighted that she is talking such high-level gossip with me. Coggins is the director, the top luminary. Although the only thing he's ever written is a scholarly book, a dialectical analysis of writer's block, everyone is afraid of him. Even Billy Reese.

"Is he in a hospital?" I ask.

"Hell, no. He's jerking off in his room right this second."

I look at her, aghast. I can't decide if I like her or not, if she's a good guy or a bad guy.

"Well, thanks," I say, feeling stupid.

"Sure," she says. "Don't worry. Eric's needed something like this. I mean—a bully, a fight. There's altogether too much feminine influence in his life."

"I guess I see what you mean," I say, and I do see what she means. I only wish that life were easier—that thirteen-year-olds with lesbian mothers and hip, dead fathers didn't need their noses broken on top of everything else.

But life is not simple, I tell myself as I walk among the black-eyed susans, the goldenrod, the Queen Anne's lace. These past few days, I have ignored, as always, the simple gorgeousness of the countryside. A regenerate naturophobe, I have not turned to the mountains, their coolness, their wetness, their concreteness, for comfort and purification. Instead I have smoked marijuana and befriended exuberantly people I might not, after all, really like. Why am I so reluctant to let the bird's songs reach me? Why am I afraid to lick the sappy bark?

Dover is alone in the room and he hasn't seen Eric since last night's trip to the emergency room.

"Why didn't you get me?" I ask. "To go to the hospital?"

"It was goddamn late at night, Mandy, and how many fucking people does it take to drive someone to the hospital? Sondra came along. I like her. What a waste of talent."

"Her talent might not be wasted. Women aren't so unlovable."

"Lovable?" Dover says. "I loved a woman once. I didn't *like* one thing about her. She was dumb, too skinny, shaved her armpits every goddamn hour. But I loved her. So what the fuck good did it do me?"

"What happened to her?"

"She's a Sufi dancer now. She dances and sells carnations in airports."

"Did you dump her?" I ask.

"Of course I dumped her. We couldn't even talk English together. All she did was whine and chew Quaaludes."

"But you loved her?" I ask.

"So I loved her, Mandy. Big deal. Love doesn't change anything. Even you know that."

"*Even* me?"

"Well you're young, Mandy. You haven't gotten really fucked over yet. Wait till you really get it up the ass. Then, talk to me about love."

"How depressing," I say.

"Yup. How's your old man? Speaking of depressing?"

"He sounds okay on the phone. I'm supposed to meet him in Boston on Friday."

"Boston. Let's go to Boston *today*."

"I can't—my conference isn't till Friday. With Reese, of all people. I just found out. They posted the conference list in the dining room."

"Well, ask for your money back."

"Will they give it to me?"

"No. But it's a fucking waste of time to stay *here*. Nothing's happening. There are no good-looking chicks."

"What about that exotica I saw you with the other morning?"

"Felicia," he says. "She ain't so much. We did it the first night."

"After I refused you?"

"Before."

"You were gonna screw *me* after you screwed *her*?"

"I took a shower."

"I bet you did."

"Mandy, don't hassle me. I am absolutely blown away by this whole fucking place. I'm splitting this afternoon. If you want a ride to Boston, meet me at lunch."

"And blow off the conference?"

"What's the point at this point? You and Reese are actually gonna sit around and analyze your rhyme schemes? Get straight, Mandy."

"You're right. But eighty dollars?"

"I'll *give* you eighty dollars to leave here with me. I know some people in Dedham who'll let us stay there. Real mellow. Decent food. A stereo. Real vegetables."

"I don't know. I want to talk to Eric."

"I really think the kid needs to be left alone."

"He's hurt, Dover."

"Goddamn it, Mandy. You're such a fucking mama. Fish doesn't need any more mamas. He already has Sondra and her cunty little girlfriend. Leave him alone. Don't treat him like some little girl."

I throw, inadequately, a paperback dictionary. It lands at the foot of Dover's desk chair.

"At lunch. Be ready or I leave without you."

I set out for the creek where Dover and Eric and I went that first night. That star-sad night when the world still seemed a good enough place—intricate, but possible. I reach into my dungarees for half a reefer and light it. The late-August wind blows coolly, extinguishing each light I manage. I stuff the roach into my mouth. Chewing paper and black-green weed, wadding it with my tongue, I realize that something is over. It is unfortunately neither my youth nor my innocence. No such luck. What is over is merely my desire to hide behind either one. Every time something horrible happens, a young nose broken squarely, an acquaintance casually killed, Jake's tortured soul newly tortured through some new orgy of self-loathing, I have retreated into false innocence, into a world that doesn't exist.

Puppets and dreams of babies' *tooshies*, special comic books drawn and captioned for Jake, little cakes shaped like frogs, sillinesses, coynesses, feynesses of all kinds. It is these props I must give up if I am to survive. I must give up the urge to cutesify the world. Cute is one of Jake's favorite words. I love it when he tells me I'm cute. But reality is what I need now. I vow to be realistic. I take in the clarity of the green-gold elm leaves, the realism of twig and branch, of knot and gnarl, of brown and yellow. No more cuteness, I tell myself. And I feel like telegramming that precise message to my beloved Jake in New York. "No more cuteness." But that telegram would be even cuter than Dynel fashioned into a skunk.

My mother told me in ninth grade that Jake's appeal was his feyness. Conscientious young girl, I looked fey up in the dictionary. One of its meanings, I remember now, is "doomed to die."

When I get down to the creek, Eric is, after all, there. He is throwing smashed beer cans, Fanta grape cans, old packages of tobacco into the creek.

"How constructive," I say.

He looks at me. He's drugged. His pupils are big as snakes' heads and just as subject, I think, to mood swings.

"You're high, I take it."

"Take it?" he says.

"I don't feel like having some hippie conversation. I'm upset."

"If you want it, take it."

"Meaning you?"

"I don't mean me." His words are as slow as a Billy Reese waking from deep, Southern slumber.

"Eric, can you talk?"

"Last night I was in the hospital. In Hildeboro, New Hampshire. If I waited any longer, my nose woulda fallen off. I'm positive."

"Where'd you get the acid?"

"It's mescalinda."

"Who gave it to you?"

"Linda. You think if somebody has bad vibes their drugs have bad vibes?"

"Nah. Who's Linda?"

"My mom's little girlie."

"Her lover?"

"Linda loves—I don't know who the fuck Linda loves."

"Eric, it's pretty hard to talk to you."

"Then come up high-er."

"I can't. I have to decide. Dover's driving to Boston. You want to go to Boston?"

"Boston baked beans?"

"Um hum."

"We can eat beans and fart. Fart in the bathtub and eat the bubbles."

"Well, I'll go ask your mother."

"No way." His eyes do turn. They hate me now. I'm ruining his trip. Do I stay here with Eric, crazy on mescaline, or do I drive to Boston with Dover?

Do I want to go to Boston because I want to sleep with Dover? Those big teeth and that thick hair? Cynicism and good sex? Jake is not a good lover. Semi-impotent unless he drinks three or four beers. If he drinks three or four beers, he usually vomits. What is the good of potency if part of its magic is vomit? A hard penis and kisses like vomit. I imagine them together and shrink.

"Mandy. Mandolin." Eric touches my face. "Is your real name Mandolin?"

"My real name is Vomit." Eric starts laughing wildly.

So wildly he loses his footing and almost falls into the creek. His laugh sounds crazed, but forced. An instant, a millisecond, before the laughter turns to limbo and then to tears, I hug him. For once my love comes in in time.

My love and its instinct make perfect sense. I am there and it's not too late. I am not too late for once to catch the first seizure of sorrow. Before the first soupy tear sneaks out of his eye, I am there to nudge it away. And the next one after that. I take off my tee shirt and Eric blows his nose all over it. Rolls it into a ball and heaves it into the water. A small eddy, the smallest eddy, the daintiest of whirlpools, carries it downstream.

"I waited for you, goddamn it. It's four o'clock, sister, and it'll be a drag watching the sun set on the fucking highway."

"I told you Eric needed me."

"Nobody needs you, Mandy. Get that crappy need stuff out of your head."

"I'm sick of being criticized." My voice is thin and whiny. I am sure Dover despises me now. I remind him of the Sufi dancer.

"Do I remind you of the Sufi girl?"

"Cheryl?" He laughs. "Forget it. Cheryl is a total space cadet. At least you're educable."

"Am I?"

"Sure."

"If I get it together do you think I can keep Jake from killing himself?"

"If you try to keep Jake from killing himself, you'll never get it together."

"What is this—Zen wisdom? Everyone is so wise today —except I feel like a jerk."

"Maybe you need a hit of Linda's acid."

"It's mescaline."

"It's not mescaline. I happened to be *raised* on mescaline."

"In the Midwest?" I ask. We both laugh. Poor Bitsy. As dumb, in a way, as they come.

"Wait a minute—"

"What?"

"*You're* tripping, too."

"Sure."

"You're *driving* to Boston on acid?"

"We dropped last night, Mandy. I'm practically crashing. And I need some reefer. Or—you have a small Valium for me?"

"Sure," I say. "Eric's getting his stuff together. I'll pack really fast. Come to my room and it'll speed me up."

"Fish is coming?"

"You don't mind, do you?"

"I thought it was gonna be a trip—you know. Me and you."

"Dover, I *told* you I can't do it."

"That was five days ago. Now we're best friends."

"My boyfriend—"

"Your fucking boyfriend has nothing to do with this."

"I want to not sleep with anyone else."

"You slept with Fish."

"How do you know?"

"Your post-orgasmal glow. Your hair looks shi-i-ny."

"Don't make fun of it. It was really positive."

"Positive? How can you fucking call sex 'positive?' Mandy, sometimes I really think you're dumber than I can ever deal with."

"But I'm educable," I say brightly.

"That's a bunch of shit. I don't know anything you don't know. It's just a line."

"A come-on line?"

"Sure. Promise to educate a girl and it's better than flowers or poems even."

"So you really got my number, Dover? If I'm so goddamned predictable, why don't you find someone better to fuck?"

"I like your perky body. And your big nose."

"It's not big. It's long."

Dover lifts my head to his head. I can feel the kiss before it comes. It is sweet as apricots and warm. His mouth is as big as the Atlantic. Or maybe it is the Indian Ocean. But Dover doesn't kiss me.

"You've had enough for one day," he says. "At least until tonight." He lets me down like a kitten gently unhinged from its mother's nipple.

We are stoned again. There is a desperateness in the air. Eric is still tripping and Dover finds it irritating that he hasn't come down yet.

"Goddamn it, Fish. How long you gonna stay up there?"

"Let's kill somebody," Eric says.

"Sounds positive," I say. "You having a nice trip, dear?"

Dover and I sit in the front seat like parents. Dover drives. I hand out bananas, beers, and advice. "Dover, be nice to Eric. He's tripping."

"Be nice to Eric—he's tripping?"

"I'll be a good mother, won't I?"

"With tits like that, you'll be the Queen Mother."

"Mandy," Eric says. "Remember when we were fucking?"

"Not now, Eric," I say.

"Yeah, now," Dover says. "I bet it was real perverted. Let's hear it."

The awful thing is, I am delighted with myself. Eric wants me. Dover wants me. Jake, who is dying, Jake who knows what madness means, Jake wants me the most.

All of a sudden, it hits me—the reality hits me as squarely as one of Billy Reese's fists. I am running away from my life. I am running away from my life. But who wouldn't? Jake could die any minute, any second. In my mind's eye I see him dead. He is wearing the Sarah Lawrence tee shirt I gave him for his nineteenth birthday. His hair is long and matted. He is lying in the earth with no coffin. His blue jeans are stained with maggots and mud. I'll save you, Jake, I say silently. I'll save you, I promise, I promise.

Inside the telephone booth, I am sweating wildly. I feel the sting of sweat as it drips behind my ear. Pillaging in my purse for a dime, I stick myself on something and scream.

"Mandy, get a hold," Dover says. I collapse into his arms.

"I have to call Jake," I say. "Give me a dime."

"In a second. Calm down."

"I have to call him," I say.

"Of course. But calm down first."

"I feel so awful about E—" I start to say "Eric," but say "everything."

The word "everything" spurts from my mouth. I collapse into coughing.

"It'll be okay, Mandy."

"What'll be okay?"

"Everything. You. Jake. Eric. Me. Everybody."

"No."

"Everything will work out."

"No it won't and you know it. I know it, you know it. It gets worse and worse and then there are funerals—"

"No, Mandy."

"Yes!" I scream. "Yes!"

"Let's drive some. You can call him later."

"If I don't call him now, when I do call him, he'll be dead."

"Why do you have so much fucking guilt?"

That word snaps me out of it. Guilt is the weakest emotion there is and yet it is all I know. Everything makes me feel guilty.

We drive into the darkness of August-turning-to-September. The air carries the scent of skunk, the smell of sulphur, the scent of skunk, the sniff of cedar, the persistent stink of sorrow.

I call Jake from a phone booth just outside Dedham. He is not coming to Boston. "Why not?" I ask. "You have to. You promised."

"Louis says I don't have to."

"What will you do instead?"

"I'm gonna try to get in at N.Y.U. For film school," he says.

"Film school?"

"I'm gonna become a director. I'm gonna be famous."

"Come to Boston. Come be with me."

"I thought you said you were with two guys."

"I'm not *with* them, Jake. I'm just with them."

"I thought you were coming back."

"I *am* coming back. I left early to meet you here."

"You—" Suddenly, the line goes dead.

Panicky, I reach the operator. She reconnects me, the line is busy.

"Break in," I say. "It's an emergency."

"No it isn't," she says.

"Please break in, it's urgent."

"No it isn't," she says.

Helpless, I leave the phone to dangle. The noise coming out of the telephone gives voice to my despair. It is an awful noise—metallic sputtering, death rattle, the sound of chains dragged across steel.

I know that Jake has hung up on me, hung up on me, then unhooked the phone. Jake hung up because he knows what happened. He knows I made love to Eric. Sometimes I think he knows everything. I think he is half an angel.

Once, in ninth grade, we were taking a walk. We abandoned the walk as soon as we came to the surburban island where we did our petting. There, in a triangle of overgrown lawn, we would lie in the grass and count the stars. Jake didn't kiss me in those days. He molested almost every inch of me, but kissing was serious and suggested real feeling. He ran his small, smooth white hands up and down my arms and back. "Now you give *me* the chills," he'd say. We pretended "the chills" weren't sexual. We pretended he touched my breasts by accident, though as time went on these accidents grew prolonged and protracted, impassioned.

"Now you give *me* the chills," he says, turning over in the April night. I reach inside three layers of shirt to feel his warm, white back. Obediently I slide my fingers all the way up his back to his neck. One finger catches on a beauty mark, a mole as black and sweetish as a hunk of Nestlé's chocolate. I feel the mole and close my eyes. In this mole there breathes his whole life. The wind rustles the maples, and the poplars are startled into a trembling. Suddenly it is raining wildly. Jake and I get up from the ground and we stand in the cold, hilarious rain. Our tryst has been upended. There is no other place to go. His recreation room or my basement —neither is adequate. We need the smell of the earth beneath us, we need the sight of the stars. Their magic is our magic, we need the stars to illumine our faces.

101

"I'll make the rain stop," Jake says.

I am fifteen years old and I giggle.

"You don't think I can do it," he says. "You have to believe in me or I can't."

"Like Tinker Bell," I say.

Jake huddles me against him. We stand under a large elm tree and I hold his hand and shiver.

"Close your eyes, Mandy," he says.

Mandy closes her eyes.

The rain stops then. The rain stops raining. Jake is an angel after all. Jake can undo the rain.

In Dedham, a large fire blazes though outside it is fifty degrees. Eric, still tripping, has started the fire. We sit, the two of us, close together, staring into blue light. I look into Eric's face. It is moony with LSD and light. I feel no love for him now. I am beginning to regret that I slept with him. I am beginning to feel just the murkiest stirrings of a kind of contempt. I fear, I fear and hate, this slippery side of my psyche. Why do I always begin to hate the people I most love?

Sometimes I lie on top of Jake while we are making love. I lie on top of him and look down into his abstracted face. His brow is tight with that bastard emotion that balances between tension and ease. Lust heaves his nostrils, quickens his breathing, jerks his body upward and towards me. He opens his cow-brown eyes to look at me. I am the woman he loves. He opens his eyes to look at me. He has reached orgasm, he feels an indebtedness, wants to give thanks to me with that look. To my limbs and my hips and my back that arches catlike, my body that contorts to please. He looks at me, then, with love as deep as dark waters, as rich as Julia Child's best mousse. I love you, speak eyes as loyal as dog eyes. In that moment I hate him so much I could kill him. Kill him or beat him or blow off his head. Or, sometimes he tells me he loves me and the words turn my stomach sick. I don't realize yet how dangerous is our love.

Later, much later, when I am grown up, I look for this love relentlessly. I stare at every man who even slightly resembles Paul McCartney. I follow cars unreasonable distances if I see a profile, or even an arm, that makes me remember Jake's profile, Jake's arm. Five years after his death, I patronize a supermarket whose meat I don't like—the meat cutter resembles Jake. Once, when I am very drunk, I sleep with a man I'm sure is Jake. I am drunk enough and crazy enough to believe it is Jake beside me. I look for Jake relentlessly. I need to touch his face.

Eric, supposedly still tripping, nods out by the fire. Dover was right in suspecting him. He was staying high as long as possible—for the attention and for the good vibes. The vibes couldn't be gooder.

There are an Afghan hound, a Doberman, and a puppy Saint Bernard. There are seven kittens from two different cats. There is a baby named Jedd and fresh vegetables, good marijuana and an acre out back.

I am holding the baby, Jedd, who goes to sleep in the daytime.

"Jedd is a night person," Sarah says. "It changed my

whole life. *I* had to become a night person. But I'm still a day person. I wake up at six no matter what. Even if I'm already up."

I laugh.

Sarah is Dover's old lover. They were lovers together in '67, and also in parts of '68. Sarah is married to Artie. Artie and Dover are out in the garden, discussing Artie's pot plants. How to keep the horny males away from the resinous females, the price of marijuana in Madison, cultivation raps.

"Are you and Dover doing a thing?" Sarah narrows her eyes.

"No," I say, "we're friends."

"And what about the tripping boy?"

"Eric is our friend."

"And how come he's sleeping in the middle of his trip?"

"He's been tripping since one midnight ago. He must be exhausted. First he had his nose broken by the biggest asshole at the conference—"

"He does look kind of beaten up."

"He's a strange person, Eric. But wonderful."

"Is he your lover?" Sarah asks slyly.

"He was once—this morning actually."

"And never again?" she asks.

"I'm in love with someone else. He's—sick."

I want to say Jake has cerebral palsy, cancer of the colon, a fragile heart. But what if Dover talked to Sarah and later she found out I was lying?

"He's mentally ill . . ." I say, trying out the words. My husband is mentally ill, gentlemen. The words sound old-fashioned, euphemistic, a phrase out of some wild domestic comedy of the fifties. Janet Leigh is explaining to the corporate board why Jack Lemmon has been acting so strange.

"I sort of don't know what I'm doing," I say. "It's making me crazy. Jake is dying. Nothing I do—" In the middle of the sentence, I giggle. Sarah must think I'm crazy. "I know this all sounds peculiar, but I've had a fairly peculiar day."

"Who do you want to sleep with?" she asks. "On the floor here with Eric or in the guest bed with Dover? I think you should try to get some sleep." It is two o'clock in the morning and Sarah is a day person.

"I'll take the bed," I say.

"Good choice." Sarah covers Eric with an afghan and shows me to the bed.

I wake up to see Dover in the grayest morning light.

"It's six A.M., Mandy."

"Why aren't you sleeping?"

"I've been rapping to Artie. It's great to be here. That conference was fucking strange."

"Why'd you wake me?"

" 'Cause I felt like being nice. I hardly ever feel nice. I wanted to be nice to you."

"Want-ed?"

"Still want."

"Like what?" I say.

"Like tell you how great you are."

"Then fuck me?"

"Goddamn you, Mandy. Forget it. Now I feel like being mean. You happy? I'll be mean. I was just fucking telling Artie how much—"

"How much what?"

"How much money I made at the races."

"C'mon, Dover . . ."

"I *can't* be nice to you. You don't like people to be nice to you. Unless they're so fucking helpless—"

"Are you meaning Jake now, or Eric?"

"Both of them."

"And you're the big strong one who's gonna rescue me from all the weaklings—"

"You know, cynicism isn't attractive in a young girl."

"What makes you think I'm so young?"

"You're used to careless men. That's not my trip. I *like* women, Mandy. I like them."

"Maybe I'm not very womanly."

"Womanly," Dover whispers.

I soften. "I'm afraid of you," I say.

"I know."

"Afraid to fuck you. I really want to. You're irresistible—almost."

Dover pats my shoulder. "Let's talk about Fish."

"What happened?"

"Yeah, Mandy. What happened?"

"Well, it was very loving."

"Well, what?"

"I don't know. What do you want to hear? All the dirty stuff?"

"No, I guess I don't," Dover says.

"Dover," I say.

"Yeah?" He is fully awake. He looks up at the ceiling.

"Tell me something."

"What?"

"Anything. What you were like when you were twenty?"

"I wasn't like anything." Dover laughs, remembering. "I was in ROTC till 1966—my senior year. Sixty-six was rough in Chicago."

"Is that when you were in love with Sarah?"

"Yeah. She was so beautiful then. She was the editor of the magazine I bought out."

"You loved her," I say.

"Sure I loved her. Every time you hear the word love, it flips you out, Mandy."

"It does. Love is all that matters to me. I take love seriously."

"Too seriously."

"Do you love me, Dover?"

"Yes, Mandy. I love you."

"Tell me again," I say.

"Uh-uh. You gotta wait for it."

"I hate waiting."

"Waiting is an important part of revelation," Dover says.

"Revelation?"

"Of finding out—you know, the truth. The Zen Buddhist monk sits under the apple tree waiting for the apple to fall on his head."

"But I would just go and pick the apple," I insist.

"Of course you would. You'd take little bites out of every apple. Even the apples with worms. That's your charm."

"But if I *waited*—" I say. "But, I can't wait. Jake will be dead if I wait."

"Jake might be dead if you don't wait."

"Either way, I lose."

"He loses. He has to live out his own karma. If he has to die, he has to die. Death isn't the end of the world," Dover says.

"Oh no? Then what is?"

"Oh, Mandy, I know it's awful. And I hope he lives and gives you everything—"

"Do you? Do you even care? You're one of those people who thinks suicide is groovy."

"No, I'm not."

"Did you ever try—?"

"Uh-uh. Never even came close. Once I ate ten Seconals and nodded pretty badly. . . . But it wasn't intentional."

"I used to think about suicide a lot. Heads in gas ovens. People jumping off bridges. But there's nothing very romantic with pills—"

"Drowning is the most painful," Dover says wisely. "Virginia Woolf drowned herself. Put pebbles in her pockets to weigh herself down."

"You make it sound pretty."

"Death can be pretty," Dover says. "Oh Mandy, you're so young and good. Life will fuck you in the ass, though, I know it. But you'll grow up to be strong and good."

"Like Eleanor Roosevelt," I say.

"Eleanor Roosevelt, but sexy."

"Do you think I'm sexy?" I ask Dover.

"Only when you talk about death." Dover gets out of the bed then and starts, remarkably, to stand on his head.

"I read this in my yoga book. It makes all the horniness go away."

108

"Why do you want it to go away?"

"Because you're not ready for me." Dover's mouth talks upside down. He gets off his head and crawls back into the bed. Outside it is growing lighter and lighter. Stripes of warm light fill the room here and there. The light shifts mechanically as the sun breaks. I could measure with a ruler the time as it passes. I could measure each moment with precise-enough tools. Dover falls asleep, the headstand has tired him. With precise-enough tools, I could measure my life.

In the morning, I am the last to awaken. Everyone is eating pancakes and joking with the baby, Jedd.

I go into the bedroom and call Jake.

"Mrs. Rinehart, this is Mandy."

"Where are you, dear?"

"I'm in Dedham, Massachusetts. Where's Jake?"

"He left for Boston this morning."

"I came here just to meet him. But I think he doesn't want to see me."

"I'll give you the number at Louis's friends."

I scribble the number on the inside of my arm. Then I call Jake in Boston.

"Will you even see me?" I say.

"Sure. C'mon over."

"When do you talk to the psychiatrist?"

"I talked to him. Forget it. I'm not going into any mental hospital."

"Did you *see* the hospital?"

"It's a halfway house—kind of."

"Did you see it?"

"Yeah. It's a house. It's nice. But forget it."

"You make it sound like I *want* you in a hospital."

"Do you?" he asks.

"No."

"Where do you want me?"

"In my hot little hand."

"I'm dying to see you. Come over."

Dover says he'll drive me to Boston. The idea of seeing Jake seems strange. It is almost as though he is already dead.

I promise Dover I'll call him. Maybe he'll be in New York for Christmas and we can rendezvous then. Eric and I have already made plans for a reunion in Central Park.

" 'Bye everybody," I say, as Dover turns the car over.
" 'Bye, you-all," I say.

"Good luck," Dover says. Jake has appeared on the front stoop. He looks small and tired.

"Jake, c'mere and meet my friends."

Jake comes down to the street.

"Hello," he says in his deepest voice. His voice was the first thing I loved.

Usually Jake tries to charm everyone. Especially people he meets for the first time. Now he says nothing, just stands there dully. Dully and tiredly he takes my arm. We retreat from the curb, climb up the stairs, enter the large and tumbledown house.

In the foyer, he holds my head like a father. He looks into my face protectively. I feel incredibly safe. It is the first time in weeks that I love him. And he is fathering me. And oh how I love to be fathered, sheltered, protected from monsters and pirates and bad guys. From responsibility and the failing of light.

"Baby," I say. "I love you."
"I love *you*," he says.
"Where's Louis?"
"Sshhh. They're inside. Come upstairs with me." The look in his eye is bright and I'm falling in love with him all over. Falling in love with his manliness, his willfulness, his pretty face, his candid eyes, his power. Jake is so powerful that loving him is addictive. I never once got enough of him, ever. Always I wanted more. I thought, at the time, twenty and younger, that love was always like this. That a kiss from a mouth you loved was determinately a dangerous descent into fire.

Upstairs he takes off my clothes. He is dressed and I am undressed. He lowers his nose into my belly. His nose is cold and my belly is hot. He kisses my belly again and again and the pleasure is fierce and infinite. I belong to this nose, this cold nose, that burrowing in the heat of my belly grows warmer and hotter and finally hot. Heating me electrically from throat to bowels. Heating me fiercely and sweetly and hot.

Andrea is a sex counselor. And, she assures me, has heard it all.

"You'd be shocked by the amount of incest that goes on every day."

"Well, Andrea—I hate to tell you this," Jake is warming to his act. "I hate to tell you, Andrea, but Mom made a pass at me the other night. In the kitchen."

"Jackie!" Andrea laughs. Only the grownups call him Jackie. Andrea is only twenty-seven, but has chosen to be a grownup.

Louis comes into the room. He's been napping. Louis loves his naps, I can tell. There is a catlike quality to him, I notice. He stretches languorously in a doeskin lounge chair. "So, Jake," Louis says. "Let's go talk."

"We can talk here," Jake says. "It's okay. Mandy knows everything. And Andrea is a *machetayneste.*"

"In-law," I explain to Andrea.

"I'm your sister, Jackie. In-law?"

"My sister," Jake says.

"I think we should talk by ourselves."

Jake looks at me and shrugs. The brothers go off by themselves.

"Jackie really loves you," Andrea says.

"You think?"

"Do I think? He's crazy about you. And he's so adorable."

"He's adorable for sure. But you know—he has terrible problems. Some of which, sexually, you could maybe—"

"He's fine," Andrea says. "All boys his age are rebellious."

"Rebellious? He's suicidal."

"*Shah*," Andrea says. *Shah* is a word that allows no argument. It is the word all grandmothers use to put the baby to sleep.

"I love Jake," I say. "I've loved him since I was eleven years old. Nobody understands."

"Understands what?"

"Andrea, he's going to die."

"Mandy!" Andrea's face turns white. "Mandy, don't talk like that."

In my mind, an ambulance races up. A doctor looks into Jake's dead eyes. Andrea looks pretty in a black two-piece suit. My mother's mascara runs down her face. The chapel is crowded with Jake's heroes. Satchmo gives Chuck a hand with the coffin. It is gleaming and polished and inside is Jake.

"I don't want to upset you, but I feel like we're all avoiding something."

"It makes sense to avoid unpleasantness. The best way to help Jake is to think positively."

"I want you to know I love him."

"You feel guilty, don't you?"

"He doesn't want to live. How would you feel?"

"Whenever I get depressed, I look at my wedding album. Do you want to see it? I brought it along to show people."

"Sure, Andrea," I say.

In the wedding pictures Andrea looks different.

"I had my nose fixed," she explains. "I had the bump removed."

I recognize some of the people in the photographs.

113

Mrs. Rinehart is wearing a pale pink dress and smiling exaggeratedly. Louis was over thirty when he finally married Andrea. It must have been exhausting to be the mother of an unmarried doctor. Probably she was accosted everywhere—in the supermarket, the hairdresser's, on line at motor vehicles—besieged by countless offers to look at snapshots of unmarried girls.

"Do you like being married to a doctor?"

"Yes and no," Andrea says. "Can you believe *I* once wanted to *be* a doctor?"

"Sure, what happened?"

"My parents wanted me to be a nurse. They wouldn't pay for medical school."

"Maybe you can do it now. How would Louis feel about it?"

"Maybe he'd be threatened. He's not so liberated, Louis. He likes his dinner on the table—hot when he's ready for it."

"How exhausting."

"It used to be exhausting. I would take his dinner in and out of the oven all night long. Now I have an electric platewarmer. I turn the thing on and forget about it. It saved my marriage, that platewarmer."

"Here," Andrea points to a photograph. "Here is Sybil Cohen, my friend whose house this is."

"She looks nice," I say lamely.

"She's wonderful. She has four kids and she's only twenty-eight."

"Do you want a child?"

"We've been trying," she says.

"I was pregnant once," I say.

"How awful," Andrea says.

"It wasn't awful, really. It hurts more than they admit, but it wasn't awful at all."

"Was it Jake's?" she asks.

"Of course it was Jake's," I say, though in reality I never knew. It could have been Jake's, it could have been Paul's from my dorm, it could have been the child of a boy whose name I never knew.

"You kids have it harder," Andrea says. "In my day, we didn't go quite so—"

"In your day, girls jumped off buildings. Bad girls had them and gave them away. Good girls killed themselves."

Andrea looks at me sharply. She thinks I only look at the bad side, but I don't. I look at the good side, too. Really.

"Mandy, try to be positive. Dwell on the nice things. You and Jake will have plenty of chances. You'll get married, have babies, everything will be lovely."

"Yes, Andrea, you're right." But Andrea is dead wrong. I will never walk down an aisle on Jake's arm. I will never have his babies. I will never sleep with him in our own double bed or keep his dinner waiting. Even if Jake survives this time, there will be a next time and a next time after that. The next time the Rineharts and the *machetaynestes* meet to listen to a rabbi's stony benediction, Jake will not be there to clutch my arm, to

115

whisper irreverences in my ear. To turn to me, and pointing at the rabbi, whisper, "You think he's Jewish?" Jake will be dead this time next year.

Jake comes out of the study then. His eyes are red and wasted. "Mandy," he says, "Louis wants to talk to you." Jake refuses to meet my gaze. He calls to the dog, Shtarker. "Come on, Shtarker," he says, opening the door, "let's run around the block."

"Well?" I say.
"He does want to die. He won't come out and say it, but it's there and we both know it."
"Lock him up," I say.
"Do you mean it?"
"Lock him up, please."
"I can't lock up my own brother."
"Then get someone else to do it."
"I can't, Mandy. I can't defy him."
"Well, how long does he have then?" My tone is bitter now.
"There's still a chance, you know."
"A chance? How can you let him leave here knowing there's only a chance?"
"Mandy, it's very complicated. I—I—" Louis is crying now. "What would you do?"
"I'd lock him the hell up."
"No, you wouldn't. It's not like giving a dog back to the pound. You can't just brace yourself, then walk away."

116

Giving a dog back to the pound? I think of Jake in a kennel full of puppies. He is teaching them how to bark to the tune of "Ain't She Sweet."

There's a knock on the door of Louis's study and Jake comes into the room. He is wearing nose glasses and smoking a cigar.

Louis and I both start laughing. In heaven, Jake will be a first-liner. All the dead people will rattle their chains.

"Enough crying," Jake says. "Louis, can we go to the airport? I want to do the act tonight. I want to get back to New York."

"Maybe we could talk again first," Louis says.

"We talked enough. I want to go now."

"Mandy isn't happy about this," Louis says. "Mandy thinks you should go into the hospital." Louis pauses dangerously. "Whether you want to or not."

"Oh yeah?" Jake says. "Is that what you want?" He glares at me meanly. He narrows his eyes and gives me a look.

I start crying then. I realize there is no escape. I can't be his lover and his friend both. I have to be one or the other.

"As your friend," I say through a veil of mucus. "As your friend," I say through a cloud of tears, "I don't want you in a hospital, but I'm afraid you'll die otherwise."

"Die?" Jake's tone is oddly ironic. "Die? Me? I'm not gonna die."

"*Now* what do you mean?" Louis says.

"I won't kill myself."

"You promise?" I ask.

117

"Yeah, I promise. Now let's go home. I don't want to miss playing tonight." Jake is still wearing the nose glasses, but the cigar lies abandoned in a mosaic ashtray. The ashtray is Israeli. There are Hebrew letters I cannot read and a design that suggests the burning bush.

"Okay, to the airport," Louis says. "Did you check the schedule?"

"There's a plane every hour," Jake says. "Let's just go there and wait."

At the airport, Andrea kisses Jake on the cheek. Then she kisses him on the mouth. Then she kisses him on the cheek.

"You two be happy," she says, emphasizing the "hap." *Hap*py. "And come visit us in Los Angeles."

"We will," Jake says. "Good-by." Jake turns to his brother. They start to shake hands, but nearly at once withdraw their hands and kiss. The awkwardness of their kiss is beautiful. Two brothers standing at the railroad track. One wore blue and one wore black. They are on different sides. Louis is the eternal doctor and Jake is the eternal patient, but beyond this they are brothers. Brothers. Two men with nothing in common except their blood and their history and a memory, perhaps, of the first time Jake rode his tricycle and split his lip on the curb.

Jake is unduly proud of his brother's achievements. It was Chuck who taught him everything he knew; Louis was both too old and too straight to have influenced him growing up. But Jake always looked up to Louis. Secure, stable, a regular guy, moral, honest, even simple. When Jake used to paste together his own newspaper in junior high school, he would excerpt technical articles that Louis had published in psychiatric journals. There among the crazy cartoons, the articles on jazz, the political commentary on the civilian review board or safety in the subways, there would appear highlights from Louis's findings on the effects of Thorazine on fetal mice.

"So I'll see you," Jake says, moving away, moving away from his brother's kiss.

"See you," Louis says, turning and taking Andrea's arm.

Andrea and Louis walk out of the airport, begin to walk back to their car. Louis turns around to get one last look at his brother, but Jake's back is turned and it is I who return the look. His back turned, Jake has missed his last chance to say good-by.

The next time I see them, Andrea is wearing a black knit dress she bought on a trip to Florence. "I never wear it," she says, "because Louis thinks I look terrible in it. He thinks I look too flat-chested." We are sitting in the chapel and the coffin is open and there is Jake, his life no longer poised on a balance so delicate it broke him.

"Oh no," I say. From where I sit, I can see just the fringes on Jake's *tallis*. White-and-gold silk drapes across his chest and he is finally, ceremonially dead. "Oh no," I say, "you don't look terrible. You look like Audrey Hepburn."

JAKE ASKS ME to go into the city to get rid of some tickets he can't use. "Just stand outside Carnegie Hall," he says. "These are a cinch to get rid of."

"Should I try to scalp them?" I ask.

"Uh-uh. Just sell them," he says.

"Should I just raise the price a little?" I tease. "To pay for my carfare?"

Jake throws me down on his bed and begins to tickle me wildly. "Scalper," he says, "my little scalper," reaching under my arm to get me. I screech and scream with the pleasure of the tickling. Lately, Jake seems to be perking up.

He'd bought tickets for B.B. King, but it turns out we can't go. Tonight is Sandy Greenwald's thirtieth birthday and we're both invited to the surprise party Chuck is throwing in her honor.

"I wish we could go to B.B. King. I hate Mimi Greenwald."

"You can ignore her," I say. "At least we don't have mothers like her."

"I hate her," Jake says.

"Well, maybe you can get out of it."

"I'll go for Chuck's sake. Chuck'd be upset."

"Does Chuck know—about—you know—?"

"Know about what?" Jake asks.

"You know—the hospital?"

"I think my mother told him."

"*That's* why you don't want to go."

"No, it's not. But I *am* embarrassed. I can't believe how I fuck up everything." Jake hits the night table squarely. "I can't even kill myself."

"But who wants to be good at killing . . . himself?" My voice catches on the word *killing*. "And I thought you promised, Jake."

"I promised, but that doesn't mean—"

"No, Jake, don't. You've been having fun lately. Last night they loved you."

Last night, returning from the airport, Jake and I drove out to the tiny club in Great Neck where Loose Leonard and Sister Jake perform their music and comedy. Jake sings in the sweetest of baritones while Leonard picks the guitar. Musically they aren't much, but their act is strangely alarming. Lately they do less and less music, more and more comedy. This change bothers Leonard because he knows he is being upstaged, and yet Jake's humor is not very humorous: He sticks a lit candle into his mouth and turns to the audience, saying, "Look—a jack-o'-lantern."

But it isn't what he says, it is only how he says it. His face is not as pretty as it once was; late adolescence has

124

undercut the softness. No longer does he really resemble Paul McCartney. Now he looks more like a
young Lenny Bruce. His eyes flash wildly, independ-
ently of his face. They seem unhinged from their delicate sockets, from the lacy weave of long Bambi lashes.
His eyes have taken on a wildness I have never before
perceived. Their glint is a glint of desperateness, and
even madness.

We meet Leonard at the club and Leonard, his lean
friend of thirteen years, has no idea Jake is unhappy, no
idea Jake is dying.

"I have a great idea, old man," Jake says. "Is Robinson's still open?"

"Robinson's? Whatsa matter with you?" Leonard
looks puzzled, but then he catches on. Something major
is brewing and I want to be part of it.

"Why Robinson's?" I ask. Robinson's is a drug-
supply company. They rent sickbeds and wheelchairs
and trusses.

"Stay here, we'll surprise you." Jake leaves me in the
parking lot. "Go inside and we'll be back soon."

Inside I see one of the managers, a twenty-five-year-
old hippie named Fox.

"Fox," I say. "How are you?"

"Hi, baby. You here alone?"

"Uh-uh," I say. "Jake will be right back. And Leonard. They want to go on tonight."

"Those two are crazy. Too crazy lately. I wish they'd
stick to their music, you know? Jake's sense of humor is
fuckin' crazy."

"He's avant-garde," I say.

"What?"

"Avant-garde. You know, sophisticated."

"*Sophisticated?*" Fox gives me a look. "What's sophisticated about dropping your pants? You weren't here last week. Jake fucking dropped his pants."

"You're kidding?"

"I mean he had drawers on, but still. He's crazy."

"But you like the music, don't you?"

"Well, they aren't exactly bringing the crowds in."

"But you're not even paying them."

"I suppose." Fox and I sit down together. Our knees touch, but we do not speak.

Then there's this enormous noise from behind the stage where Thai Stick is setting up their equipment.

"What the fuck?" the lead singer says.

"It's Jake," I call out apologetically. "You know—the washboard player."

"Well, tell Washboard to cool it. We're testing the amps."

Backstage, I see Jake and Leonard dressed in lab coats, seated in wheelchairs. Jake is spraying Leonard's hair white, and Leonard is simultaneously gluing cotton to Jake's soft chin.

"We're Pops and Higgenbottom," Jake says, looking up from Leonard's head.

After Thai Stick finishes their set, Jake and Leonard come out. They have gotten carried away. There is so much cotton glued to their faces, so much white hair, so much white lab coat, all the audience can make out in the darkness is two pairs of glinting eyes. One pair glints right at me. There is hilarity in those eyes, and love.

126

"Well—hello—there—Higgenbottom." Jake speaks in the thinnest, most arthritic of voices.

"What?" Leonard answers.

"What?" Jake says.

"I can't *hear* you," Leonard says.

"What?"

"I can't hear-r-r you."

And so they continue for fifteen minutes. The audience hasn't laughed once, except for a retarded man who sits in the corner holding his groin.

"Mandy," Fox whispers. "How the hell long is this gonna go on?"

"Don't you think it's funny?" I ask. "Don't you think they're brilliant?"

The audience is full of fifteen-year-old girls with stringy blond hair, high on diet pills. Their boyfriends sit on the opposite side of the room chewing on Valiums they've filched from their mothers. Occasionally one of the girls goes over and sits with her boyfriend, but soon she shrugs her shoulders, arches her back, shakes her tiny titties in disgust. No wonder they sit apart from each other—the boys are down and the girls are up. On the stage, Jake and Leonard are still wound up in a fantasy no one understands.

"What's that, Pops?" Leonard cackles.

"I can't hear-r-r you," Jake whimpers.

"They loved you last night," I say, running my fingertips across his brow. Lately his forehead is always too cold. My finger finds it damp now, and chilly. Slightly, I cringe. "They loved you at the Mandala."

"You kiddin'?" Jake says. He chuckles. "Fox told me to forget it. Either play music, the regular stuff, or don't come back."

"But they love you," I say. "The audience loves you."

"I hate the way you have to lie about everything. Why do you do it, Mandy?"

"I don't," I say.

"You know you do. You and my mother both. You always have to make believe things are better than they are."

"Maybe that's what women are supposed to do."

Jake looks at me then. His eyes are incredibly Russian in this moment. Our mutual histories speak in this gaze—icy tundra and the sound of hooves, Cossacks slapping the sides of horses. Our great-grandmothers sit over tea, pale steam ushers forth from the samovar. His great-grandmother Rachele snorts with laughter at something my great-grandmother Gittel has whispered. The borscht grows thick in the cast-iron pot and outside it's the nineteenth century and cold.

I was born to love this boy, to love him, to prod him gently over the border from boyhood to manhood, to make him a man. To listen to his dreams of greatness, laugh at his jokes, kiss his face, receive and fulfill his seed. His ancestors carried this seed delicately over the frozen and hostile terrain. Pushing milk wagons soft with eiderdown, noisy with candelabra and prayer cups, they made their way to Brooklyn and hot dogs, to vaudeville and the ILGWU. And my relatives, having made this same trip, met his relatives in dairy restaurants, in brassiere factories, in balconies where together they clapped for the glory that was the Yiddish stage. Or maybe they read one another's angry letters in the *Forvertz*. Or laughed at each other's jokes over babka. Or embraced at a service commemorating the New Year. "Next year in Bel Ridge," they might have joked at the end of a Passover service. "Next year in the Promised Land."

And all of their dreams came true. Except one. This Jacob would be the last of his line.

I sell Jake's tickets easily outside Carnegie Hall. I approach a young Black guy dressed in red, green, and black.

"Wanna see B.B. King?" I ask.

"You givin' something away?"

"No. The tickets are six fifty each."

"I bet I could get ten tonight."

"You could."

The guy buys the tickets and I'm all through. I have a few hours to kill before Jake meets me at six. He's at the psychiatrist's now and won't be done for a while.

I walk downtown to a coffee shop and sit down at the counter. Next to me sits a very handsome man with a sheepskin vest and a beard that matches. I open up my *Village Voice* and start reading a movie review. But I can't forget the man sitting next to me. He smells of the woods, the New Hampshire woods. He reminds me a little of Dover.

129

After a while we are talking together about *A Clock-work Orange.* I say something about the Russian forms Burgess used in the novel, but by now I've lost him, I'm over his head. Over his head and under his groin. In my fantasy we're locked in an embrace so passionate I.Q.s have ceased to matter. "Wanna go sit down on the steps over there?" He points towards the 42nd Street Library.

Seated there on the library steps, we watch the pigeons eat hot-dog rolls and together take stock of our passion.

"Come to my place," he says and I follow. Down the subway station steps, then the D train to Fourth Street. We take the train ride in unportentous silence. I continue reading the movie review, remember that Jake hated *A Clockwork Orange,* that the sex and the violence disturbed him.

"Why are they making sex so violent?" Jake asks me one night while we're watching T.V.

"Sometimes it *is* violent."

"How about with us?"

"Sometimes I feel violent."

"Like what?"

"Like I want to—I don't know."

"But you never feel like hurting me?" he asks.

"No," I say, and he pats my knee. "But sometimes I want you to hurt *me.*"

"No you don't," he says. "No, Mandy."

"Sometimes I think I'm a masochist. That I'd get off if—"

"No," he says. "You're my girl." Jake holds me

130

wrapped around myself. My position is fetal and I need to be soothed.

"Let me tell you," I say. "Don't not listen to it."

"Okay," Jake says. "Like this?" He punches me in the arm.

It hurts, but I start laughing. Jake has so completely misunderstood. How could anyone think S & M meant punches in the arm? How could he have thought that's what I was afraid of? How could anyone have ever been so young?

The stranger walks up the steps of an apartment on Barrow Street. He looks less pretty outside the restaurant. Possibly he's over thirty. What am I doing here with this man when I'm in love with Jake? Aren't I still a nice girl? Why does a nice girl pick up a man in a coffee shop while four miles away, uptown at the psychiatrist's, the boy she loves is dying?

The stranger takes off his clothes. "You do me," he says. "And then I'll do you."

Why don't I run away?

His body is offensive to me. He does not feel like Jake. He feels like scabs under my fingertips, his breath is sour milk.

Jake is supposed to meet me at six. Riding the subway back uptown, I listen to the conversation of three small Spanish girls. They are fourteen years old and giggly. Boldly they smoke cigarettes, applying and re-applying lip gloss between each husky puff.

Outside the Huntington Hartford, Jake stands alone in the September rain. I see him first, but when he sees me, he begins to jump up and down. Wildly he bounces in the light rain, his curls flapping around him.

"Let's go see a movie," he says.

"I don't want to."

"There's three Buster Keatons at Lincoln Center. We could see one and still get to Chuck's—"

"I don't want to. But I sold the tickets. To a scalper," I say. With the word scalper, I start to feel dizzy. I imagine an Indian dancing wildly, the scalps of young Jewish girls dangling from buckskin. And the bloodiest scalp is mine.

Jake and I sit down at the edge of the park. He looks at me and I'm crying. "What happened at Dr. Nold's?" I ask.

"He says I don't need to be in a hospital. I *knew* I wasn't crazy." Jake brushes a fingertip under one of my eyes, then the other. This is the way he stops my crying.

"*Now* why are you crying?"

"I love you, Pooch," I say.

"I love *you*, Poochess." These were the pet names we used at fourteen. Now I am twenty and undeserving. The stranger's sperm starts oozing out of me. Or maybe I am imagining this. The rain grows heavier and begins to drench us. My hair turns wetter and wetter. I begin to shake with the cold. My hair grows wetter, my foreleg grows wetter. Now I am not imagining anything. Jake holds me tight against his slicker. I smell wet rubber and

132

heave and heave while the stranger's seed travels down
my leg, ending its journey inside my shoe. Maybe torrents of sperm will come out. Torrents, rainstorms,
bucketfuls, floods. Jake will ask me what it is—why is
there such a puddle beneath me? What is this endless
supply of strange fluids that issues forth from the
woman he loves? And after the deluge, what? What
then?

"I went to bed with somebody," I say.
"When?" he asks.
"At the conference."
"I knew it."
"I knew you knew it."
"But why?"
"I'm not good enough anymore." Now we both are
crying.
"Who was he? One of those cats—you even made me
meet him. That older cat?"
"No, the young one."
"You're kidding, Mandy."
"No, I'm not kidding. And I hate myself so much."
I wish that Jake would get angry. I wish he would
sock me in the mouth. Instead, that old and familiar
resignation crosses his face, turns it gray, takes all the
roses out of his face, all the light from his eyes.
Jake slams his head against the back of the bench.
"Hit *me*," I say.
Jake slams his head against the bench.
"Hit *me*," I plead.
"It's my fault you went to bed with him."
"How is it your fault?"

Jake lets out an animal sound. The sound of pain and regret and surrender.

"I *told* Nold you went to bed with some guy."

"I knew you knew," I say foolishly, as if praising his insight. As if that were the point.

"Nold says it's time I knew the truth about women."

"You're kidding," I say. "A psychiatrist said *that*?" Brightly, I try to change the subject. But the subject will not change.

"So why, Mandy? Tell me why."

"I don't fucking know." My voice grows angry, defiant, rebellious.

"And now you're mad at *me*," he says. "Well why'd you go fuck some young guy? Do you love him? You want to marry him?" Jake thinks he's funny.

"I want to marry you," I say.

"Well, let's get married."

"Okay," I say. "When?"

"Would you marry me right now—this second?"

"Yes," I say. "Yes."

"Do you really love me?" he asks.

"Yes," I say. "Yes."

"Well, we're already married anyway."

"Why are you being so nice?"

"Because you feel so bad and I hate it. And guess what—I bought you a present." Jake takes out a ring.

"Not now," I say. "I'm not good enough."

"Now," he says.

"Not now. Give it to me when we're happy."

"I'm happy," he says.

* * *

We walk across the park to the subway. We get on the train and travel in silence to Brooklyn where Chuck and Sandy live, where they live and grow old together, in love, husband and wife, for real, forever.

Walking into Chuck and Sandy's living room, I am sure everyone knows I've just screwed a stranger. Everyone knows except Jake. The smell of the stranger's seed takes over the entire atmosphere. Even Mimi Greenwald's perfume isn't strong enough to kill the smell. In every corner, I smell sperm. Any second a noisome puddle will form on the Aubusson carpet, will issue forth from my faithless womb and soak the birthday guests' feet. The immediate family, the good friends, the *machetaynestes.*

"Surprise!" we all scream as Sandy walks into her own living room. Perhaps if she'd known about the party, she might have fixed herself up. Her ratty wet hair reassures everyone this is indeed a surprise.

"Darling!" Mrs. Greenwald shrills, digging one fingernail into Sandy's neck. "Why don't you go in there and make yourself beautiful?"

Sandy gives her mother a witchy look. "And now!" Mimi says sternly.

Jake and I look at each other, horrified. Sandy starts to cry.

"It's my birthday," she says foolishly. "It's my birthday." Mimi looks at her daughter in disgust, dismisses her with a stubby hand. As the hand, Mimi's hand, flaps down in disgust, two gold bracelets rub metal.

Sandy sulks off into the bedroom, where she takes off her clothes and gets under the sheets. Jake and I follow her in there. Jake is the world's greatest cheerer-upper. He gets down on his fours and starts barking at Sandy. And Sandy laughs and I laugh and soon she ushers Jake out of the room so she can get dressed again.

"My mother isn't a bad person," Sandy says.

"Of course not," I say. "There's no such thing as a bad mother." I mean what I say, more or less, but the words sound insincere.

"But what am I supposed to do about my hair?"

"Blow it dry," I say.

"It takes hours. Absolute hours to dry."

Sandy looks in the mirror. "My mother wanted me to get a nose job. My Uncle Murray's a plastic surgeon. Uncle Murray would have broken my nose practically for nothing."

Someday we'll be sisters, I think. Jake and I are getting married.

"I bet my mother wishes I would get a nose job, too. When I had my teeth fixed, my mother wanted the dentist to break my nose while I was under."

Sandy laughs.

"Mothers," she says, adjusting the shade of her face.

136

Orange liquid she swirls around in circles across her cheeks. "I have more pimples than brains," she says. "And I'm thirty years old today. Thirty. Can you believe it?"

"I bet it's nice to be thirty. I'd love to be thirty."

"Why?"

"You're married and you have Garth and a nice apartment and—"

"And a great rug, right? That fucking rug owns my soul. My mother keeps threatening to remove it. I encourage the baby to spit up on it. Maybe I could get him to do a number two. . . ."

We giggle. Mimi comes into the bedroom. *"Now* don't you look nice," Mimi Greenwald says. "Why don't you do something with your hair, though? Wrap it up in a nice piece of cloth. Do you have a nice oblong, darling?"

Just as I seem to have recovered my humor, Jake gets really depressed. He is sitting in the corner holding the baby when I come back into the living room. Mrs. Rinehart, busy inserting candles into sheet cake, winks at me as I sit down at the feet of her youngest child.

"Whatsa matter, baby? You thinking about before?"

"Uh-uh. Well, a little," Jake says. He adjusts the baby's position. "Now *this* is the fontanel," he says, "the softest part of a baby's head." Jake is always giving me baby lessons. When Garth was first born, nineteen-year-old Jake read the entire Dr. Spock.

"Fontanel? You made that up."

"Uh-uh," Jake says. "I'll bet you the forty you owe me and double it—that it's a real word."

"The forty?" I ask. "I thought forty dollars was forty days. Will I lose my forty days if I lose the bet?"

Jake looks at me, pained. Now why did I bring *that* up?

"I've been thinking," he says.

"Don't do *that*."

"I've been thinking we really *could* get married. I'm twenty and a half," he whispers. "Other people do it."

"Just greasers," I say. " 'Cause they have to."

"Well, who cares? Let's get married."

"Our parents would kill us."

"We'll do it secretly, then tell them."

"But I want a *real* wedding. With a rabbi and a *chuppa*—"

"A rabbi? Mandy, you're nuts. If there's one person I can't stand it's Rabbi Davidowitz."

"There's other rabbis," I say. And there are, and plenty of them. And yet as life is cruel and ironic, as life is relentless and dumb, it is Rabbi Davidowitz who stands finally over Jake's brand-new bones and recites the eulogy.

"Get Mimi," Mrs. Rinehart says, nudging my shoulder. "We're ready for the cake."

Back in the bedroom, Sandy is crying again. All I can hear is the word "selfish" issued from Mimi's frosted lips. "Selfish."

"What?" Mimi addresses me sharply.

"Mrs. Rinehart says we're ready."

138

"Well, tell Annette we're *not* ready. Not the least bit."

"Mo-th-er, it's my birthday. Now leave me alone. Get out of here!"

Mimi and I leave the room together. Walking next to her through the hallway, I notice I am a head taller. She stinks of L'Air du Temps, and I stink, still, I dread, of sperm.

The cake is lit, everyone's singing, but Sandy hasn't come out of her room. The party's been going on for an hour and the birthday girl still hasn't appeared. Jake hands me the baby, goes in there, sweeps Sandy onto his shoulders and carries her into the room.

As the final strains, and strains they are, of "Happy Birthday" fill the room, I can hear Mimi whispering to her son-in-law. "Selfish," she repeats. "Selfish."

Sandy and Chuck embrace and Chuck proposes a toast to Sandy's beauty. I'm not sure if I'm imagining it, but I think I hear Mimi repeat the word "beauty," and then, I think, I hear her laugh.

"A nice champagne, Manny," Ben Greenwald says. "Very light."

"Yeah," Manny says. "A whole case I brought. It's New York State, but that's the new thing. Domestic instead of French."

"I'll drink to that," Ben Greenwald says. "To domestic champagne," Ben toasts.

"And domestic bliss," I say, raising my hand, and

along with my hand, raising the hand of the man I love. Everyone turns to look at us. We are young and healthy and so much in love. Everyone turns to smile at us. Jake is holding the baby and I am holding Jake.

"To me and Mandy," Jake says, then, raising the baby in the air. "To me and my wife."

"Wife?" Mimi Greenwald says. "What?"

"He likes to call her that," Annette says.

"Why should he call her his wife, she isn't his wife?"

"They're in love," Annette says. "In love."

"Love, schmov," Mimi Greewald says. "I still don't understand why—"

"Quiet, Mimi," Ben Greenwald says, finishing off the last of his champagne. And miraculously, Mimi falls quiet.

On the way back to Bel Ridge, Jake and I nuzzle in the back seat while Manny drives and Annette talks.

"We were all in such a good mood," Annette says. "Till the Vulture started in. Poor Sandy. No wonder she's neurotic."

"Sandy's okay, Mom," Jake says.

"You didn't *used* to like her."

"That's 'cause I was upset Chuck was marrying her. I was just a kid. But now I like her. She's cute."

"Cute?" I say.

"Sandy's a cute girl." Cute is Jake's favorite word.

"I thought *I* was the cute girl."

"You're the cutest," Jake says. He kisses me. Mrs. Rinehart watches the kiss in the rearview mirror. The kiss is passionate, but it doesn't disturb her. Anything

Jake and I do is okay these days. It used to be she'd get mad at us whenever she suspected sex. Now, sex is one more way of keeping her son alive.

Once the three of us watched together a television show about V.D. It was she who'd asked me and Jake to watch it. During the commercials she looked at us closely, cross-examining our expressions. Her message was clear: Fooling around leads to disease, unless, of course, you're married.

This attitude toward sex was the only thing that ever made me uncomfortable around her. And yet everything had changed weightily since Jake's suicide attempt. No longer did she hang out in the bathroom, within easy earshot of Jake's bedroom. She used to arrange, I fantasized, to arrange towels for hours. Jake and I would see her at the linen closet when first we'd go into his room, locking the door behind us. Hours later, when we'd emerge, giggly and silly and spent, she'd be holding the same circus-striped bath towel, pretending to furious absorption.

I wanted to say, "That's the same towel you were holding two hours ago. You can't kid us, Mrs. Rinehart." She wanted to say, "You can't kid me, kids, no matter how brushed and tucked-in you are when you reemerge from that room." But neither of us said anything until after Jake was dead.

Sitting in the family room, Annette still wearing the same tweed suit she'd worn to the funeral one week before, I told her how much I'd loved him. And woman to woman (finally I was grown!), I admitted that Jake and I used to make love. "You must have felt really guilty," she said. "You must have felt really bad."

We sat there long after the mourners had left, and Mrs. Rinehart knit squares. "I can't even do the afghan without him. He used to help me with the colors. Tell me what matched nice with what." Annette Rinehart has impeccable taste, Jake's was only so-so.

We sit in the November afternoon. It is the seventh and last day of mourning. Jake is as dead as a dead Diehard battery, its warranty mislaid. My soul can provide no charge. The final answer to the question—if love *is* a question, curious and shy—is another question, natch. Will my life ever find a meaning apart from this meaning? Will death and its awful, civilized smell follow me everywhere I go? Will everything I touch turn to death and ashes? Is Jake better off without Jake? His soul now free to find consolation and warmth in some spiritual land?

My favorite version of heaven is a Yiddish resort where Jake sits in lawn chairs, drinking tea out of old *Yortzeit* glasses. His grandfather sits beside him, his nose buried in the *Forvertz*. Jake and his Grandpa Samuel hold hands. They don't talk much—just an occasional joke or anecdote. Maybe the one about the tailor who could only fit humpbacked women.

Samuel bites open a pumpkin seed and remembers

142

the smell of old Hungary, the goats' creamy milkings, the crackle of boots on straw. Jake recalls 1957 and a Colonial house on a shady street. There is Kerri Mandel on roller skates, her key glinting silver around her neck. She topples down onto the asphalt of the driveway at Pennington Road. Falling, she shows the world her *tooshie*. Jake is astounded to see it. He squeals.

"Grandpa, remember the time Kerri fell down in the driveway? And her *tooshie* was bare?"

"A thing like that an old man doesn't remember. But there was another girl once, also with a bare *tooshie*. In 1907. In Budapesh it was. . . ."

Annette finishes a pumpkin-colored square, tosses it onto the couch. The ten o'clock news is interrupted by a public service announcement. "It is now ten o'clock," the announcer intones. "Do you know where your children are?"

"I know exactly where he is. He's under the ground," Annette says.

Manny misses the Bel Ridge exit off the Long Island Expressway.

"I'm sorry, Annette. I was thinking—"

"Of what, Manny? You didn't used to be such a thinker." Annette touches the back of Manny's bald head. And Jake and I smile in appreciation.

"Soon you go back to school?" Annette asks.

"In a week," I say sadly. Jake and I haven't even talked about my return to school. Physical distance isn't

143

the problem. Bronxville is only one train ride out of Manhattan, two trains and two subways from Bel Ridge. Physical distance isn't the problem, the problem is the divergent directions our lives are increasingly taking.

I will go back to school to write dreamy sonnets, argue in Hegel seminars, attend lectures on subjects which Jake alternately finds funny or threatening. He tells me he isn't smart enough, that I'll fall for a philosophy professor. Some vaguely hip Bertrand Russell in blue jeans who will refer to our lovemaking as a dialectic.

"No, no," I tell him. "I want to marry you."

Jake once took a philosophy course, trying to find out what appealed to me about, say, Kant's *Prolegomena*. To him it was all gibberish, he hadn't a pompous bone anywhere. And at twenty I have only pompous bones— a pompous patella, a pretentious parietal, a pedantic sesamoid.

Jake wrote me a letter the spring before he died, expressing in true Jake-like fashion his final thoughts on the examined life: "I think, therefore I get nauseous," he wrote, and signed it, "Love, René."

What appealed to him ultimately about my commitment to the conceptual and the arcane was that it was, at bottom, cute. "Woody Allen's first wife," he assured me, "was a philosophy major, too."

I love Jake more than I've ever loved anyone and beyond that I love him more. But twenty years old, I do dream of intellectuals, of men who aren't bald at twenty, of men who are so strong *I* get to break, *I* get to flip out, *I* get to do the crying. I want to be the family hysteric. I want to throw the fits, take the overdoses. I want the attention, the coddling, the reassurance of a stronger person. I don't want to spend my life trying to get him out of bed, looking for him when he disappears, deserts his child bride and all her brats because he cannot cope.

Once I told him a story about my Aunt Etta. It is the saddest family story I know, and as a child, my favorite. Uncle Max married Aunt Etta and they had six babies and were very poor. Aunt Etta was a wonderful woman —never bitter, never petty, and also a famous jokester. Once she awakened her daughter in the early morning, screaming, "Wake up, Pearl! Your hair's all fallen out!" Everyone was devoted to her.

Etta raised her orphaned brothers and sisters, saw that their wives and husbands were fed. One morning, Max leaves to pick up a pumpernickel and by evening he is whistling on top of a freight car, dreaming his way to Scranton. At sixty, Aunta Etta is still hemming brassieres and taking home eighty dollars a week. One day Max walks in and it's twenty years later. Within the week he dies and Aunt Etta's life's savings buy him a funeral to which the brothers and sisters come, but only for the pleasure. "He came back so she should bury him. He came back only to die."

"When I grow up, I'll be just like Uncle Max," Jake says brightly. We are only fifteen years old and he finds the story oddly romantic.

145

The sad thing is that he was right. Perhaps I am lucky my Max will leave me while I'm young enough to recover. Before he gives me babies to feed, and rent to pay, and regrets. Perhaps his death will save me from a life of disappointment. The deeper and greater the passion, the more severe the regrets. If Jake dies now, will I have a better chance? If Jake dies now, will chance die with him?

We are sitting in the family room. The parents have gone to bed. "I have something to tell you," Jake says.

"I have something to tell *you*," I say.

"You first," he says.

"No, you."

Jake gives me a serious look.

"Okay," I say. "I fucked somebody."

"Besides that young cat? Fish? What a name."

"Besides him. Today. I went to Carnegie Hall and I sold the tickets. And then I went to a coffee shop and I met this—"

"Today, Mandy? Today?"

I nod at him dully. "Today. We went to his room and it was awful. It was something I had to—"

"Why today?"

"I don't know, Jake. It's not even like I wanted to—"

"Then, why?" he says.

"I don't know. But I'm the one who needs the psychiatrist. I'm the one who's crazy."

Jake grows quiet after that. The rest of the night I want to explain why I have gone to bed with the stranger, but when I open my mouth to tell him, words can-

146

not come out. There is somewhere a reason for me to humiliate myself. And beyond that, there are reasons to humiliate myself further. There are reasons for me to suffer. I have not suffered enough.

"Well, what were *you* going to tell *me*?" I ask.

"I don't want to now."

"Are you punishing me?"

"No."

"We're both in this together," I say. "For better or worse. You might as well tell me everything."

"Leave me, Mandy."

"Leave you alone?"

"No, leave me. Now. And don't come back."

"You can't break up with me," I say. "I'll never go away. If you think I was annoying in ninth grade, wait till you—"

"Mandy," he says. "I realize now what I'm doing to you. I realize and I can't—"

"No, Jake. I don't care how bad it gets."

"But I still want to kill myself. And I'm going to do it. And we both fucking know it. And I *will* kill myself. I *will*. No matter what I say to you, no matter what. I'm going to be dead soon."

"I'll kill myself first, then."

"No, you won't."

"You think you can fucking do whatever you want. But—goddamn you, I hate you. I hate you." I am kicking Jake now. I am kicking his legs, his shins, his ankles. I am kicking his knees and I would like to kill him.

"Then do it now," I say. "Kill yourself now. This

147

second." Every muscle in my face is tensed, but then Jake starts to laugh.

"C'mon, Mandy." Jake holds me then. He holds me against his warm chest and he smells like creamery butter and wool and lambs eating alfalfa. Goodness must be the name of his smell.

"You *are* going to do it, aren't you?" I lift my head from his chest to say this, but he pushes me down into fragrant wool. "You are, you are, you are." My words are muffled by his body. It is into his chest that I speak over and over the sad words of my love.

It is five o'clock in the morning when Jake drops me off at my parents' house. He has agreed not to kill himself until the next time I see him. Until the next day at ten o'clock when I'll accompany him to the doctor, and this time, finally, meet the man who thinks Jake doesn't need to be locked up.

I let myself into the house, where I see my mother huddled in a chair with a copy of *New York* magazine. She is half-asleep and the magazine lies open across her knees. She is reading about the entertaining strategies of Carter and Amanda Burden.

"Ma," I say, "it's me."

"Uhmmm," she says. "Mandy?"

"You weren't waiting for me, were you?"

"Uh-uh," she says. "How's Jake?"

"He's—Ma, he says he's gonna do it."

"Kill himself?"

"Yeah. I mean he took it back, but he means it. I

148

think he should be in a hospital. And I *told* Louis he should be in a hospital—"

"You can't tell everyone what to do, Mandy. Especially a doctor."

"But I'm right, Ma. He's doomed."

"He isn't *doomed*, Mandy. He's only twenty years old. He doesn't even know what life *is*."

"Whadya mean, Ma? He's old enough to die."

"It will pass, Mandy. My father used to say to me, 'This, too, will pass.' And that's what you have to tell yourself every day. Life is not easy for anyone. I know what it means to be miserable."

"But you aren't crazy. Jake is crazy."

"Schizophrenic, you mean? Two different personalities?"

"No, Ma, he's not schizophrenic. At least, I don't think he is—"

"Well, he's probably not really crazy. I feel sorry for *you*, though, Mandy. You didn't even know what you were getting yourself into. . . . I remember when he was fourteen and he came over in a blue parka—with a hood. Remember that coat?"

I smile.

"And he seemed so young. The both of you seemed too young."

"Too young for what? To be in love?"

"Well, that, too. But too young to always be so intense—"

"Were we intense then?"

"Were *you* intense? The two of you were always fighting and *you* were always crying. But I could tell, even then, you had a great love. There is something so special about that boy. But you—you're the golden girl."

"Tell me more," I say. I sit down on the brocade sofa. I pick up my mother's hand and hold it.

"Ooh, your hands are cold," she says.

"Tell me more about me and Jake. When we were young," I say.

"Well, he was wearing that blue parka with the hood up. And he had a beautiful deep voice even then. And he was so tiny, I couldn't believe it. How little you both were. And I remember he shook my hand and said, 'I'm Jake Rinehart, how do you do?' He had beautiful manners," she says sadly.

"And did you like him?" I ask.

"Of course I liked him. But I knew he'd drive you crazy. And he did. And he still is. Try to stay away from boys who will drive you crazy," she says.

"How can you ever tell?" I ask.

"Oh, you know what I mean. You need someone strong, Mandy. Someone who will answer all your questions and let you—give you—satisfaction. You are a person who needs her satisfaction."

"Well, what about Daddy? Did he give you satisfaction?"

"I don't remember," she says. "You know your father. He was always the same."

"But did he answer your questions?"

"I'm not sure I had any questions. I was a different kind of girl."

"What did you love about him?"

"He was the most romantic person I ever met. He always wore sunglasses. Even at night. I thought he was glamorous."

150

"But why did you marry him? Did you like it that he was an artist?"

"I liked his tan. He had a great tan."

"You didn't marry Daddy for his tan!"

"Oh yes, I did. But that's not why I love him now."

"Why do you love him now?"

"I don't know. Maybe because he's not a fool. And besides, he thinks I'm great. Listen, Mandy. I'm not you. You're going to be a great woman. You're very special," she says.

"*You're* special," I say. "And what's so special about me?"

"You're the golden girl," she says vaguely. "My golden girl. And you'll find some golden boy . . . some wonderful, brave person . . ."

Ten o'clock in the morning and I'm late for the psychiatrist appointment. Jake must have gone without me. I call his mother, who tells me he never came home the night before.

"Is he with a girl?" she asks. Her voice is tinny and empty. "Is there another girl?"

"I don't think so. Maybe he's at Leonard's."

"I've called Leonard, I'm almost ready to call the police."

It's happened. Jake is dead.

It's not possible. Today we would go and see the psychiatrist. The three of us would talk about my infidelities. The psychiatrist would marvel at my incredible insights into myself, my singular lack of self-pity. My instinctive moral sense and the fact that I'm the most full-of-shit person who ever walked the earth.

"Call Dr. Nold."

"I already have," she says.

"Why didn't you call here earlier?"

"I spoke to your mother early this morning."

"I love him," I say incongruously.

"I have to keep the line free," she says. Does her voice hold the sound of disgust? Has she finally found me out?

"I love him," I say again, senselessly.

"Mandy, I'll call you back."

My sister Leslie sits in a kimono eating Captain Crunch.

"Hi, Leslie," I say, patting the top of her curly head. She looks up from *Eohippus*, the local purple rag. Leslie's espresso eyes brim over. She cannot look at me and not cry. Leslie's life is not easy either. She is withdrawn and sad at sixteen, and wise. Another special child.

"So, did they find him?"

"Uh-uh. And his mother asked me if there was another girl. I know it's an emergency—but still—isn't that kind of intense?"

"Ummm," Leslie says. Her hands, her tiny prehensile hands, rest now on my knees and she gulps. She understands Jake's pain better than I do. She is more like him than like me.

"What is this—a French whorehouse?" My father comes into the room. "Still in your nightgowns at ten-thirty? What are you, a couple of whores?" My father's words are familiar as buttons. He has asked us for years to get dressed before breakfast.

He grabs Leslie's foot. "Owww . . ." she snarls indignantly.

"Where are your slippers?"

"I don't have any slippers," she says.

"I'm sure you do," he says. "Or wear Mommy's then. Sonia, why don't these girls have slippers?"

"They have slippers," my mother says.

My father's irrational disgust towards nightgowns, his insistence upon the wearing of slippers, my sister's fragility, her Captain Crunch growing soggy in the blue glass bowl, the bowl my mother gave her own mother for Mother's Day in the thirties. Depression glass, they call it. Everything I have always counted on is still rampant around me. My family is an endless cushion into whose stuffing I sink endlessly, endlessly sink and sink.

"Daddy, he never came home last night."

"He'll turn up," my father says. "Shit always floats to the surface," my bad-boy father reassures me.

Leslie starts to laugh.

"Conrad," my mother says, "what a thing to say." My mother starts laughing too.

"But, Daddy . . ." I say.

"There's no point but-Daddying." His voice is rough now. He can stand all this less than I can. "Shall we have some breakfast, Sonia? Or has everyone gone crazy?"

"Everyone's gone crazy," I say. "Jake is dead."

"What?" Leslie looks at me.

"Can we put an end to this hysteria? Put some clothes on." My father prods my sister in the ribs.

"Owww," she growls.

"Now you listen to me," he says, his index finger pointing straight at my Polish nose. "Hysteria helps nothing. You've got to pull yourself together. And right this instant."

"Look, Mandy," my mother says, calling from the kitchen. "I found you a nice little piece of Brie."

I spend that day looking through the college catalogue, trying to decide on courses. I'll be going back to school in six days. Soon I'll be my old self. Heated discussions of goodness and the pitfalls of utilitarianism. Seminars on the role of women in capitalist culture, drunken revelry in the dormitories, drives to Manhattan at five in the morning to satisfy a collegiate craving for fried won ton or fresh croissants.

For the first time in weeks, I feel a sort of elation. I love going to college, I love to theorize, I love to drink too much, I love the ivory tower more than any other home. I will go back to school and have riotous fun, amaze my professors, and fall in love. Fall in love? Fall in love? Fall? In love? With whom?

The phone rings and it's Chuck. "He's here. He's fine," Chuck says wearily.

"Where was he?" I ask.

"Walking around the city, he says."

"Can I speak to him?"

"Mandy, he doesn't want to talk to you. I don't know why."

"Well—tell him I love him. But, Chuck—is he dead?"

"No, he's fine. I said he was fine."

"Is he hurt?"

"No, Mandy. I have to get off—"

"Be good to—" I say as Chuck clicks off.

Jake won't speak to me for the next three days, and finally I stop calling his house. I feel just a little relieved. I use the time to get ready for school and to mourn for the end of the summer. The end of summer always hits me hard. In the middle of New York blizzards, I fantasize about heat. I love it when it's one hundred degrees and the sweat pours down and everything sticks. It drives my father crazy when I turn down the air conditioner, refuse to sleep with a fan. My parents start complaining as soon as the mercury hits seventy.

"Can you believe this heat, Sonia?" my father asks my mother, though it's seventy-three degrees and April. "Get ready for a heat wave."

My mother fans herself languorously with the *Bel Ridge Buy and Sell.*

"I'm a touch cold myself," I say and I put on a pair of woolly socks, dreaming about real heat, smoke coming up from asphalt, a dozen eggs frying on every block.

My parents exchange looks as I ease on one sock, then the other. Unnatural child, they think.

* * *

My sister Leslie and I drive out to the shopping center on a panties expedition. After heat, new panties are my favorite consolation. I like nothing more in the world than a hot day in July and a whole new batch of panties.

"They were talking about you last night," Leslie says. Although Leslie is sixteen and has only a learner's permit, she does the driving. I hate to drive.

"Mommy and Daddy?"

"Yeah. They're worried about you. They think you're gonna get crazy from this stuff with Jake."

"He won't even talk to me now. What did they say?"

"Daddy said he didn't think Jake will kill himself. But it's bad for you to be so depressed."

"What do *you* think, Leslie?"

"I think he should do what he wants."

"Do you ever get suicidal? I used to worry about you a lot."

"That I would kill myself?" she asks.

"Yeah. When you were thirteen and everything was so crazy for you—"

"Thirteen's a bad age," Leslie says wisely.

"Twenty is worse," I say.

"Not for me it won't be," she says. "It could never get that bad again."

"Did you feel crazy?"

"Sometimes. I hated myself so much. And I couldn't talk to anybody. Everyone thought I was just surly, but the wo—nothing made sense."

"Did you ever think about how you would kill yourself?"

"Pills, I guess. That would be the easiest."

"They say men shoot themselves in the mouth because it's the most reliable. But women care too much how they look."

"I couldn't stick a gun in my mouth," Leslie says.

"Me neither," I say. But I think then of a cool pistol, silvery, elegant, all curves. I imagine the barrel sliding down my throat, the flick of a finger then, and a noise. I see my face burned up with gunpowder and blood gushing out of my ears. I see myself dead in a crude coffin that resembles an orange crate. Jake stands above me crying. Rabbi Davidowitz recites the prayer for young Jewish girls who have shot off their faces.

"There's Adler's," I say, and Leslie makes the turn-off.

Inside Adler's we buy panties, scores of panties, and we both feel much better.

It is the morning of the day I am to leave for college. Jake still hasn't come to the phone. I have walked past his house and peered into his bedroom. I saw him once, in the half-light, in profile. I saw his dark eyes and the shape of his curls.

I lie in bed, sweating, and fantasize that Jake is locked up. He is locked up in a cage full of monkeys. The monkeys make faces at one another and furrow their paws in their relatives' fur. Jake is happy in the monkey cage. He doesn't have to bathe or groom. The female monkeys love to care for him. One female monkey in particular has taken a special shine to Jake. She likes the feel of the hair on his head and she likes the hairlessness of the rest of him. She likes to knead his fleshy back and the beauty marks there intrigue her.

Tourists come to the monkey zoo. There is Mimi Greenwald, gauche in a leopard-skin suit! Wearing leopard skin to the zoo is like offering a Talmudic scholar a lamp whose shade was rendered from his *tante*'s own thighs. But Mimi is oblivious to this lapse in taste. She offers the monkeys an orange, an orange proffered from a hand encased in the thinnest kid. Jake's wife, the largest female, snatches the orange, and with it, the glove.

"You naughty monkey!" Mimi calls out. "Ben, that monkey took my glove!"

"There are other gloves in the world," Ben says. "Don't worry, Mimi. I'll buy you new gloves."

Mimi stamps her foot, then squints, recognizing Jake. "Ben!" she screeches. "We're in luck. Guess who's here. Jake," she whinnies, "*you* do something. *You* get back my glove from that ape!"

"That's my wife, Mimi. You better be careful what you say about my wife."

"Again with the wives. Jake, you're impossible. Get me back my glove!"

Jake toddles up to the far end of the cage and pokes his hand between steel bars. He grimaces wildly at Mimi Greenwald, then lets out a growl so primal and beastly a clamor goes up among the monkeys, amidst the cats, amongst the bears. The whole zoo is joined in an awful chorus of howling. Of wailing and puling and growling and blating. Jake plucks the other glove from Mimi's hand and tosses it to his monkey wife.

* * *

158

"Mandy, it's nine-thirty. Don't you think you should get out of bed?" My father's voice sallies up the stairs and interrupts my dreaming.

I'm all packed and ready for the drive to Bronxville when Jake pulls into our driveway. His face holds only pleasure as he walks up the flagstone to kiss me.

"I'm mad at you," I say.

"It doesn't matter," he says.

"Whadya mean it doesn't matter? It matters to *me*."

"I mean we shouldn't be mad at each other. We should just kiss and make up."

"But you were horrible. When Chuck called and you wouldn't even come to the phone . . ."

"Mandy, I couldn't."

"What do you mean you couldn't?"

"I was fucked up. On pills."

"Oh, God."

"I took one pill like every half hour. I wasn't trying to—"

"Oh no? What were you doing?"

"I don't know. I walked all the way from the George Washington to the Brooklyn Bridge. When I got to Brooklyn, I could hardly stand up. So I took a cab—to Chuck's."

"Did you go to the hospital?"

"Yeah. But no one knows except Chuck and Sandy. They're even gonna pay for it, so I don't have to put it on Blue Cross. I don't want my parents to find out. And I had my stomach pumped. That part really hurt—the pump. Then I split."

"How long were you at Chuck's?"

"A day or two, but I felt ridiculous. The Vulture came over at one point and I had to hide in Sandy's closet. That was really funny. . . . And Mrs. Greenwald actually took away their rug. That nice rug that was in the living room? Mandy, I'm telling you, it was the funniest day of my life."

Jake and I hug then. It is impossible not to forgive him. Again he almost killed himself, but again he is still alive. I think of that famous line attributed to Dorothy Parker—the line about her promiscuous suicide attempts: "If I keep on doing this, one of these days I'm going to really hurt myself." Legend says she wore pink satin ribbons to obscure corrugated wrists.

"Oh! It's Jake," my mother says, as we walk into the living room. "How are you feeling, dear?"

"I'm fine, Mrs. Charney."

"Do you want some coffee, dear?"

"Okay."

My father comes in and the four of us sit down to coffee. I love to hang out with Jake and my parents. I love it that my parents like him. Jake and my father love to talk about vaudeville and it's great when they really get going. And life can be so good when it's good. And life can be so possible.

"Did I ever tell you about the guy in the Village who dresses up like a Clorox bottle?"

"What about that *tweed* skirt, Mandy? Does it need to go to the cleaners?"

"What about that guy with the chickens under his hat? Have you ever seen that guy?"

"What happened to my *other* denim skirt?"

"Jake, have another small piece of cake. Or maybe

you want some tuna fish? Or ice cream? The ice cream is really good."

Jake promises to come up for the weekend. He kisses me long and sexy even though my father has already turned over the car. I kiss him and make him promise he'll come up in a few days. He says he's even thinking about registering for school. He has gotten into N.Y.U. film school, things seem to be working out. N.Y.U. is practically as good as Sarah Lawrence, he says. Now he can feel like my equal. He won't have to worry that I'll fall for Bertrand Russell in blue jeans. I won't fall for anyone except the man I love.

"Be good, Poochess," he says. "I brought you something," he says. Out of his pocket he takes an odd-looking piece of plastic.

"What's that?" I ask.

"Remember when I got beat up that time? At the Automat? In tenth grade?"

"After the Arlo Guthrie concert?"

"Yeah, it was Arlo. Well, this is a piece of the hat I was wearing the night they beat me up."

"That was a hat?"

"It was Chuck's lifeguard hat. I loved it. That's why they beat me up. They didn't like my hat."

"Mandy, your father's waiting," my mother says.

"Mandy, your mother's getting hysterical," my father says.

"You better go," Jake says.

161

"Do you want to come along, dear?" my mother asks Jake.

"No," Jake says. "I have to go to Manhattan. I'm gonna register for school."

"*That's* nice," my mother says.

"Well, I didn't say I was gonna *go* to school. Registering's the only fun part."

"Well, maybe film school will be more fun," my mother says.

"Maybe I can join a fraternity," Jake says dreamily. "And eat goldfish," he says. "Now eating goldfish is the kind of thing I can relate to."

My father smiles at Jake. My father was just as rebellious in his day, as alienated as anyone. My father could match his wildness of old against any modern-day Holden or Brando. He used to jump from rooftop to rooftop in his boxer shorts.

"Good-by, little Jake," I say, as the Cadillac shifts into gear, as Claire the bulldog lets out a yip from her place in between my parents.

"Good-by, Mandy. I love you."

"Come up this weekend," I say.

"I will. I will. Good-by."

By the time I get to the lobby of my dorm, there's a phone message from Jake. While my parents carry up six boxes of books, seven suitcases and a pole lamp, I sit in the phone booth and talk to Jake.

"I can't do it," he says for the seventh time.

"Do it anyway," I say.

"I don't want to be in school. I can't even understand

the catalogue. I can't read, Mandy. How can I take real classes? I'm too dumb."

"Jake, you know you can do it."

"I don't want to," he says. "I'm through with school. Forever. I can't do it."

"What do you want me to say?"

"That we can get married. I'll come up and get you tonight. We'll drive somewhere beautiful and have a pre-honeymoon orgy. I'll bring the dirty playing cards."

"Do you really mean it?"

"Yes, Mandy, please."

"Say you're only kidding."

"I'm not kidding," he says.

"Okay. Come up soon."

"I'll be there with the moon," he says.

"Come sooner. I have a million things to do."

"Wear something white," he says.

"How about my tennis dress?"

"You don't play tennis," he says.

"I do a lot of things you don't know about." And then I realize what I've said. "I meant—I was only being mysterious."

"You didn't fuck anybody, did you?"

"Uh-uh," I say. "I was just being mysterious."

"Well, don't be so mysterious," he says.

"Okay, I better go. My parents have moved all the stuff themselves. They're probably going to kill me."

My father comes down the stairs of the dorm, sweating profusely. His pink oxford shirt is soaked all the way through, the sweat on his forehead has curled his hair.

"I'm sorry, Daddy."

"Why did he call so soon?"

"He misses me," I say.

"Tell me, Mandy. What is it?"

"I think he needs me there. With him."

"Well you have to be *here*. You have work to do."

"I know that, but if you love someone—"

"If you love someone, you respect what they have to do."

My mother comes down the stairs then. She appears a little disoriented. "I just saw that girl from Texas. That pretty girl. What's her name?"

"Georgine?" I ask. "Georgine Martinson?"

"She's not really as pretty as you," my mother says.

"Who said she was?" I ask.

"But a beautiful girl and she told me she was marrying some boy from Dartmouth."

"I bet he's an asshole," I say.

"Nice language," my father says, feigning boredom.

"You want to go somewhere, Conrad?" my mother asks. "Let's all go have a cup of coffee."

"Is Daddy mad at me?" I ask my mother while my father pauses behind us, sniffing at the air. "Because he had to carry up all that stuff? Because Jake called me as soon as we got here?"

"Your father isn't ever mad at you. He's worried," she says.

My father catches up with us. "It smells remarkable here," he says. "Don't ever underestimate the importance of smells." He smiles at me then. His gaze is fatherly, protective and kind. And oh how I love to be protected. It is practically my favorite activity.

We are sitting in the campus coffeehouse, drinking

cappuccino and laughing. My father gestures at the group of boys sitting at the next table. They are giggling audibly, discussing the campus production of *The Homecoming*.

"At least Jake has no competition," my father says. "Are there any *men* on this campus?"

"They're practically all gay," I say, "but so are a lot of the women."

"Really?" my mother says.

"Let's face it," I say, "everyone is becoming bisexual."

"I'm not," my father says. "I haven't given it the least bit of thought."

"Maybe Georgine could find you a date. A Dartmouth man," my mother says wistfully. "Do they still have those Winter Carnivals?"

"C'mon, Ma. Get off it. I hate Georgine and so would you if you knew what she was like."

"That's not the point, Mandy. Maybe she could find you some serious student—a philosopher."

"I'm in love with Jake and I don't want to go out with anyone else. And why are you pushing Protestant fraternity boys at me all of a sudden? All of a sudden you want me to marry some asshole Protestant boy in a sweater."

"So only Protestant boys wear sweaters," my mother says. "In my day, Jewish boys wore sweaters, too."

Our table falls silent then. We were having such a good time and I had to go and ruin it.

"I'm sorry, Mommy. I don't know why I got so upset. But I'm not going out with anyone. I want to be faithful to Jake."

"Faithful?" my father says. "Faithful?"

"Figuratively speaking," I lie.

"What Mandy meant," my mother says, "was—"

"Don't tell me what Mandy means. Mandy means what she says."

I look at my father then. And then I look at my mother. They are really worried about me. They want to root for Jake, but they can't. To root for Jake is to root against me. They only want me to be happy. I can dig ditches if I want, chuck my college career, become a world-famous junkie if it suits my fancy. They only want me to be happy. They know that Jake can't make me happy. They know that Jake wants to die.

"Well," I say, clearing the air, offering a choice bit of gossip to make up for before. "Well, guess who's famous for screwing every boy she can get her hands on?"

"Not you, I hope," my father says drolly.

"Georgine?" my mother asks.

"Yes, and she's the biggest hypocrite who ever lived. She sat in the living room once talking about how she wouldn't ever have sex before marriage because how could she do it and not get a little present from God. A little present from God, could you die? And she begged Michael Glatstein to let her go down on him."

"Really?" my mother asks, her eyes as dark as chocolates. "Really," she says.

"Mandy, don't you think you could learn to talk like a lady? I hate intellectual girls with foul mouths."

"Look who's talking, Daddy. You use curse words I never even heard of."

"Yeah, Conrad," my mother says. "You do have the

dirtiest mouth. Daddy has the most *graphic* descriptions," my mother says. "When he describes someone, later you can never think of them without getting nauseous."

My father relaxes finally and smiles. He is the naughtiest boy of all.

"Tell me about Georgette and Michael Gladner," my mother says.

"Georg*ine*, Ma. Georgine."

"All right, Georgine."

"Well, Michael Glatstein—you know who he is. He ate dinner with us once in the dorm."

"Intelligent-looking?" my mother asks.

"Yeah. With terrible skin. Well, he came into her room once—she was wearing only a pair—"

"Do I really have to hear this?" my father asks. "Do we really have to talk about *shiksa* underwear?"

Alone in my room, I feel safe. If ever I was good at anything, I am good at being a student. I like to study. I like to be lectured to. I like to sit in the library surrounded by shelf upon shelf of wisdom, the old books, their crackling bindings, the gifts of books made to the college in the names of so many who died too young. Chain-smoking, scribbling down notes, treating myself with the literary quarterlies and a Tab from the machine after four hours of hard-core Hegel, then I am in my element. Then I am truly free. And I savor those long, wet nights when I sit safe in the library, warming my bones with metaphysics, knowing that this world cannot last, that this world is not at all real.

167

Doesn't everyone, after all, talk incessantly about the "real world" and what it's like out there? And I read the *Myth of Sisyphus* and I read Durkheim and Alvarez, and still suicide doesn't materialize, suicide isn't real. It's like seeing the Sistine Chapel, suffering one long, breathtaking look, then heading straight for the postcard rack because the postcards are more real. Just so, even as I love him, I slip away from Jake's dying, I avoid even imagining the terror of his pain. I turn to Sartre and Camus instead. Except Sartre is chipper at seventy; Sartre didn't cash in his chips when he was twenty and brazen. Everybody wants to die, isn't that the secret?

And what about death anyway? Maybe it isn't so scary to die. Dover said it wasn't the end of experience, but how much hippie bullshit is that? Reincarnation upsets me far more than it comforts. I am sure that when the time comes for me, I will be ready to rest. The idea of dying one day and coming back the next—perhaps this time as a Negro houseboy in antebellum Georgia—or can one only go forward in time?—the idea doesn't lend comfort. And who would Jake come back as? A toilet comedian? A saint? A perfect child delivered to the world to redeem it of its sin? Didn't he once make the rain stop raining? Could he possibly be the Messiah, that spirit towards whose imminence the Jews left holes in their strawy roofs? In case maybe He should show up and feel too bushed to use the door?

"Man-n-dee, it's me." A girlish voice at the door. Georgine. "Man-n-dee, can I barge in?"

"By all means," I say.

And there she is, as redheaded and bubbly as a red herring in a glass of seltzer, the herring pushing irrelevantly, but persistently, to the top.

"Georgine," I say. "My mother tells me you're finally engaged."

"Well, I have the ring and everything."

"Let me see it," I say. Georgine shows me the ring. The stone is as big as her nose, but her nose is, after all, tiny. And even though she is five nine, so are her feet. "Dougie loves my tiny little feet." She actually said that once. But Dougie is out of the question now. Abandoned in some Princeton common room, he and his fellow victims sit and reminisce soulfully about their days with Georgine.

Secretly, Georgine is compelled to suck off every Jewish man who comes within ten feet of her. And that's why she likes me. Maybe I'll explain to this professional strawberry blonde what it is about Jewish men that makes her want to eat them.

"Mandy," she drawls, "I met this boy. Earl would just die if he knew—"

"Earl?"

"Earl's my fiancé. You'll just love him. He's witty like you. Poetic."

"Dartmouth?" I ask.

"Alpha Delta Phi. And an absolute saint."

"You mean he takes your shit?"

"Mandy, that ain't even fair. I've been gooder than a nun, I promise. But I met this boy—I didn't even sleep with him—"

"But you sucked his cock."

"Mandy, don't be crude."

169

"Well, you sucked it or you didn't suck it. Which?"

"You are *impossible*. I came in here to show you my ring, and because you're special."

"Special? You mean Jewish?"

"No, I don't mean Jewish."

"Well then, what the hell *do* you mean? You are addicted to Jewish come and you want me to explain it to you."

"Mandy, I just give up! I came in here because I saw your little mother—"

"My mother is *not* little," I say, realizing how ridiculous this discussion has become. It is like trying to talk straight to a deaf Doberman.

"Georgine, I like you. Even though I think you are highly weird, I like you. I have no idea in the world why you find Jewish boys irresistible. Maybe you could seek professional help. . . ."

"Mandy, you don't have to be so condescending."

"You're right, Georgine, I don't. But I'm fucking pissed off at you coming in here and telling me about all the Jewish boys you sucked off. You don't understand how insulting it is."

"I love the Jewish people," she says bravely.

"Well, why are you marrying Earl? Maybe you should become a social worker and suck little Jewish boys from underprivileged backgrounds."

"Don't think I haven't thought about not marrying Earl. I don't even like his you-know-what. It has this rubbery—"

"Georgine, I've heard enough! Enough!"

"Don't you want to hear about the first time we did it? It was so moving, Mandy. I pretended and it worked. . . ."

170

"You pretended to come?"

"I pretended to be a virgin."

"And old Earl bought it? Good for you."

"He gave me the ring, didn't he?"

"He sure did. And I only hope he doesn't give you anything else."

"You mean a little present from God?"

"That or the clap."

"Mandy, you take the romance out of life."

"I wish," I say sadly. "Now get your bottle of you-know-what out of your little closet. I'm in the mood for a drink."

"I got so drunk one night in Fort Worth—it was a very special night. . . ."

"Get your bottle, Georgine. And then I'll listen to all your stories."

Jake is on the downstairs line. I get buzzed in the hall, and then I go down.

"Jake," I say. He is halfway to Bronxville, but has stopped off mid-route to call me. "Jake," I say.

"Do you still love me?" he asks.

Georgine and I drink a quarter of a bottle of Haig & Haig. Georgine prefers Chivas Regal, but the Haig & Haig comes free because her father is on the board. We drink Haig & Haig and ice and smoke up her Kools. Why do so many redheads smoke Kools? Does it come with the territory?

Georgine is sloppy now. She has taken off her shirt, though her motivation is not clear. Perhaps she is simply the kind of girl who feels at home in a brassiere.

"This is the same brassiere I was wearing the night Earl first squeezed 'em." And then she collapses into a fit of giggles.

"Tell me about his you-know-what," I say.

"You don't even care," she sulks.

"About his you-know-what? I do too."

"I'd tell you except you don't care. You don't care who I marry."

"I do care, Georgine. I'll even dance at your wedding."

"No Jews allowed," she drawls, and then she starts laughing again.

There's a knock at the door and Jake comes in. Jake sees Georgine in her black brassiere and his eyes light up with boyish delight.

"I made it," he says. "After I called you, the car ran out of gas. I had to call Triple A."

"Call AA again!" Georgine says. " 'Cause I'm just drunk." Then she looks down at her white chest, her freckles and her black brassiere. "Ooooh," she says and turns around to put on her parrot-green sweater.

"Did you have a nice summer, Jake?"

"Not especially," Jake says. "What about you?"

"I had an incredible summer. Incredible." Even though she has her back turned, we can tell that she is arranging her breasts.

"I demonstrated cosmetics at Neiman-Marcus and I fell in love with Earl and now we're all engaged."

"Mandy and I are thinking of tying a knot," Jake says.

"You're kidding," Georgine says. "You're kidding. How incredibly touching."

"Not *the* knot," Jake says. "Just *a* knot. In one of Mandy's sneakers."

"Oh you," Georgine says. "I thought you-all were serious. What did you-all do this summer?" She bats long lashes in Jake's face.

"I took a survival-training course," Jake says coolly.

"Survival?" Georgine says. "What's that?"

"They leave you in the woods with three matches and a hit of LSD."

"Really?" Georgine asks. "You wouldn't take LSD, would you, Jake?"

"Sure wouldn't," Jake says. "It's no good for you."

Once Jake took so much LSD when he was sixteen that he tripped for five days. I wonder whether Louis blames his mental problems on acid. Now Jake doesn't even tolerate marijuana. Lately he's become so straight I sometimes don't recognize him.

After Georgine leaves the room, we crawl into the narrow cot. We lie there with our clothes on, our feet locked, our eyes staring up at the ceiling.

"I want to get married tomorrow. We could drive somewhere tonight. We could go to Niagara Falls. I'd love that," he says. "Have you ever been to Niagara Falls? We could rent a barrel and go over together."

"I have to *register* tomorrow. You have to go back and register, too."

"I can't. I missed the R's. The R's were today."

"You can register late."

"I don't want to go to school. I want to get married."

"Even if we got married. What would you do then? Just lie around and be married?"

"That sounds great," Jake says.

"And who would pay the rent?"

"We could live right here in your room."

"Get married and live in a dorm? That doesn't sound very fun."

"Well, I could get an apartment, I guess. But then I'd have to get a job."

"What kind of job could you possibly get?"

"I could be a truck driver."

"That sounds really depressing."

"I could make French fries in one of those baskets. I even know how to do it," he says.

"That sounds even worse."

"I could ask my parents for money. I bet they'd give us tons of money if we got married."

"You could work in the delicatessen."

"Uh-uh," Jake says. "I can't work the slicing machine. I'd cut my wenie off."

"But you *could* work in the deli, you know?"

"It makes my father nervous, I think. And I always have to fuck off at a job. You can't really fuck off when your father's the boss."

"But you could eat corned beef all day long."

"That reminds me," Jake says. "My mother gave me some food for us. Halvah and some roast beef."

"Let's eat it now," I say.

"It's our honeymoon food," Jake pouts.

"Are you being serious—or what?"

"About getting married?" he asks. "I want to marry you," he says.

174

"But you don't want to get a job. And you don't want to be in school. Getting married isn't going to give you something to *do*."

"You don't want to marry me, do you?" He averts his eyes from the ceiling now and gives me a melting, a dusky gaze.

"*Eventually*, I do," I say. "It seems ridiculous now. We can't live in the dorm, married. It doesn't make any sense."

"When's eventually?" he asks.

And I remember there is no *eventually* when you'e in love with a dying man. Is this, then—his proposal—is it a dying man's request?

When we were little, me and Leslie, we used to play a game called "Dying Man's Request." By the rules of the game, no matter what the dying man requested, you couldn't say no.

"Eat three spoonfuls of Noxema," Leslie would say sternly. "Yecch," I would say, "uh-uh." "Dying man's request," she would say solemnly, and I, knowing the rules of this dead-serious game, would eat the three spoonfuls, or at least lick up enough of the stuff to satisfy the gods, and Leslie.

And here in my bed was a real dying man with a reasonable enough request.

"If you get a job," I say, "or something. I'll marry you then," I say.

"Why be sensible?" he asks. "You think being sensible makes things work out, but it doesn't."

"Then what does work out?" I ask wearily.

"Nothing works out," he says.

We lie in the bed for several hours. We eat up all the honeymoon food. We make love and when we are finished, dawn is breaking through September sky.

"Let's go somewhere," he says. "I don't want to hang out here. Colleges depress me."

Everything depresses you, is what I want to, but do not, say.

"Jake, I just *got* here. And now you want me to leave."

"You have the rest of your life to be in college."

"And what the hell does *that* mean?"

"Nothing," he says.

"Yes it does. It means plenty. You're manipulating me. Passive-aggressive," I say.

"Look, Mandy, I don't need another goddamn psychiatrist. Everyone wants to be my fucking psychiatrist."

"I don't," I say. "But you're secretly implying you're not gonna be around for long. That's a form of manipulation."

"Who've *you* been rapping to?" Jake sounds startled. "I hate it when people start psychoanalyzing me."

And then I start crying. Another form of manipulation, but surely I'm too young to know this. When I start crying, Jake is always nice to me. He loves to make me cry, but not out of sadism. It is the same as with my mother. My hypersensitivity, or merely my eternal willingness to cry, reminds that the heart is also a muscled organ, that the heart has its weight to toss, and toss it will.

"All right," I say, smiling. "Let's go somewhere. And if we feel like getting married, then we will."

IV

JAKE LEANS OVER ME and buckles my seat belt.

"I never wear a seat belt," I say.

"Wear it now," he says. "For me."

"Why do you want me to wear a seat belt? You never used to care about seat belts."

"Today is a special occasion," he says. "Today is your wedding day."

"That doesn't make sense," I say, but I am getting tired of arguing with him. I keep the seat belt buckled to please him, unsure of what he intends. I think he is acting weird on purpose. Today is my wedding day?

Jake turns on the radio, switches the tuning dial back and forth. He switches and switches, but nothing sounds right.

"Leave that on," I say. "I love those call-in programs."

"No," Jake says. "I want to listen to Sid."

"But Jake, Sid isn't on anymore. You know they took him off the air."

"I don't care, " he says. "I want to listen to him anyway. I want to hear his theme song *now*. I *need* to listen
to Sid, Mandy."

"Oh, Jake," I say. I take his tousled head in my arms.
I poise his nose against my breast. "I think I understand about Sid. First your grandfather dies. Now this.
You feel it's like a conspiracy, don't you? You think the
whole world is trying to—" He looks up at me and his
eyes flash danger and fear. Understanding threatens
him.

Jake sits grimly at the wheel. I try to make him
happy. He always loves it when I sing because I sing so
badly. "There I go, there I go, there I go . . . pretty
baby. Everytime I'm near you, I really can't complain.
I'm in the mood for love." Jake smiles weakly, thinly.
He looks at me like he hates me for trying to make
things better.

We are on the Major Deegan now and we are stuck in
commuter traffic. Jake is in no mood for traffic. Persistently he tailgates the car ahead. Following too
closely. For years now, Jake has been guilty of following
too closely.

He looks at me with a crazy dread in his eyes. "I can't
stand it, Mandy."

"The traffic?" I ask.

"The traffic, Sid, my grandfather, you . . . I think I'll
just—" He taps the car in front of us. A woman turns
around in the back seat of the car ahead. She wags one
swollen finger at Jake.

182

"Who does she look like?" Jake nudges me. "Who does she remind you of?"

"One of the Lennon Sisters?" I ask.

"C'mon," Jake says. "I'm not in the mood for fooling around."

Jake taps the car again, but only slightly. The nose of the Rineharts' Buick nudges the wide-bumpered fanny of the silver Bonneville. This time three ladies turn around—three matching ladies, their hair the color and texture of gauze cooked in egg.

"*Three* Mimi Greenwalds," he says, tapping the car a third time. The ladies turn around again. Their identical mouths pout in three separate moues. They are all saying "sue" or else they're all saying "you."

"Mimi Greenwald has *black* hair," I say.

"You know what I mean. You can still tell they're bitches. I want to fuck up their car."

"Jake, you're being crazy. It's not the ladies' faults we're stuck here. And I think you're really getting sort of obsessed with Mimi Greenwald. It's weird. Mimi Greenwald isn't your enemy after all."

Jake looks at me, stunned. Apparently, Mimi is the enemy. Or else, Jake is really starting to flip out. His depression is one thing, his withdrawnness I can handle, but if he starts getting truly *crazy*, I'll—but what *will* I do? I can't leave him, I can't break up with him. I'm here, stuck in this traffic, for life. Or at least till the end of *his* life—and the way he's acting he *might* die before the traffic jam clears.

The traffic does ease up then, and luckily for us, the Bonneville swings over to another lane. I am convinced that had we stayed there behind the ladies five minutes longer, Jake would have rear-ended them within an inch, or less, of their lives.

Ten miles farther down the highway, Jake is still threatening the ladies under his breath.

"Are we going to Niagara Falls?" I ask him meekly.

"We're going to Manhattan first."

"I thought you wanted to get married."

"Maybe," he says. "But that isn't really what you want. I can tell you don't want to marry me."

"I never said that," I say. "It's just I'm really mixed up."

Outside the car window, the world is vanishing quickly. Jake is following too closely, but the world is vanishing nonetheless.

In Manhattan, Jake pulls the car into a parking lot. He turns off the ignition and then he touches his hand to his breast. "I think I'm having a heart attack," Jake says quietly.

"C'mon, Jake."

"A heart attack, Mandy. A real live heart attack!"

"You aren't having a heart attack. We didn't sleep last night. You're tired."

"I'm not tired," he says, "I'm dying."

"What do you want me to do?" I ask.

"Call the psychiatrist."

"Really?" I ask. "You really want me to?"

"Call up Dr. Nold," he says, "and tell him I'm in a parking lot and my heart is going too fast. I don't want to die, Mandy. Let's get married before I die."

"Let me hold your hand," I say. "And I'll tell you a story if you want." Jake's brow is sloppy with sweat, his eyes are fixed in an empty stare. His hand rests fast on his heaving breast. He is counting the beats of his heavy heart.

"*Feel* it," he says, pushing my hand onto his hand, pushing my hand against his heart. "Doesn't it feel weird?"

"I can't tell the difference," I say. "I don't know what to feel *for*. Maybe you're just feeling panicky. Can you take a tranquilizer?"

"I'm twenty years old," he says. "In three months I'll be twenty-one. And what the fuck is the point?"

"Of life?" I say. "I don't know, baby."

"You're a philosophy major," he says. "What do they teach you in all those classes? You must know something. You're the smart one," he says.

"I think I'm the dumb one," I say.

"You're the best there is," he says. And then he starts to laugh.

"What's so funny?" I ask. "Are you laughing at me?"

"They make us do all these things. Go to kindergarten, take out the garbage, kiss the lady in the bakery . . ."

"Your parents?" I ask. "Are you mad at your parents?"

"My mother loves me. She doesn't even think I'm crazy. She just believes all the doctors because she's Jewish."

"The doctors don't think you're *crazy*, Jake. They

just don't know how to deal with you. You try to kill yourself one minute, then tell the doctors you just want to sleep. What can they do? And then when they want to lock you up, you won't let them."

"Whose side you on, Mandy?"

"Whose side are *you* on?" I ask.

"I'm rooting for the Brooklyn Dodgers," Jake says. The life has come back to his eyes.

"The Brooklyn Dodgers don't exist. Now it's the L.A. Dodgers. You know they don't have the Brooklyn Dodgers anymore."

"See what I mean, Mandy? You think I'm crazy, but if you just pay attention, every time you turn around, something is gone. First, my grandfather, then Sid, now the Brooklyn Dodgers."

I looked at him. He has forgotten his heart. His heart is beating regularly again, if ever in fact it beat otherwise. His heart is capable of anything—Jake finds love in the strangest places—his heart is capable of anything, but not arrhythmia. There can be nothing wrong with Jake's heart.

"I know," Jake says. "Let's go see Mrs. Kopke." For some peculiar reason, Jake wants to go visit his nephew's baby nurse.

"Is that what you feel like doing?" I ask.

"You don't want to," he says.

"I didn't say that," I say. "But why Mrs. Kopke of all people?"

"I like her," Jake says. "She's cute."

"I went to college yesterday and now I'm back in the city. I thought we were going to go somewhere. You said you wanted to get married. I'm supposed to register today and so are you. How can I possibly get anything done? You act like—" And then I stop. Jake looks at me, stunned.

"Okay," he says. "I'll take you back to school. I'll leave you alone from now on."

"That's not what I want either."

"Then what the hell *do* you want?" Jake asks.

"I feel like we're going around in circles. I feel like I'm not getting anywhere with you."

"What do you want, Mandy? I thought we could have fun today."

"You ignored me for a whole week. A whole week you wouldn't even come to the phone. I wanted to talk to you. I walked past your fucking house. I looked into your window just to see your fucking curls."

"My curls are still here. Look at them now."

"You're sabotaging me," I say. "You don't want me to be in school."

Jake looks damaged. I have hurt him for real.

I close my arms around him. "This is crazy," I say. "I'm sorry."

"It's okay," he says. "We're both crazy."

We sit in the parking lot and kiss. There is nothing else for us to do. We kiss in the parking lot for hours. Both of us know there is nothing left but kisses and reminiscence and death.

"I'll take you back to school," Jake says.

"What are *you* going to do?" I ask.

"I'll go back to N.Y.U. and try to convince them to let me register."

Back on the East River Drive, Jake stops the car in the middle of the lane.

"I can't drive," he says.

"You have to drive," I say. "Someone's going to hit us." Cars approaching from behind squeal their brakes crazily, honk, head for the back of the Rineharts' Buick as if they intend to hit us. At the last second, the cars swerve right into the slow lane, but how long will the cars accommodate? How long can Jake misbehave so badly?

"Mandy, call the psychiatrist. Tell him I can't do it."

"Drive off the exit. There's no phone booth here."

"Mandy, help me," he moans. But I'm afraid to get out of the car. I'm terrified an oncoming car will hit me, but I'm even more afraid that Jake will speed off without me, hurling the Rineharts' Buick into the concrete divider. Or maybe he'll speed off crazily into the early afternoon, in search of the three matching ladies, in search of Mimi Greenwald's black spirit, camouflaged blond, in triple, to deceive.

"*I'll* drive," I say, just as a Rambler comes up behind us, squeals on the brakes, just in time. "Jake, drive. *Now*," I say. "Just drive to that exit. It's only a—"

I remember that the ambulance attendant had a strawberry-blond ponytail. I remember the taste of blood and steel. I remember Jake's arm coming close to hold me, his face gone white as some linen sale in early January or late July.

* * *

"He tried to kill me," I say.

"What else do you remember?" the doctor asks. He seems too young to be a doctor. He looks like a Mousketeer.

"Are you the doctor?" I ask.

"Yes." The doctor smiles. He feels my legs over and over, up and down from knee to toe. He strikes the bottom of my foot with an absurd doll-sized mallet.

"Jake is really vain," I say.

"Is he?" the doctor asks.

"Go look at Jake and make sure he's still—you know. If his nose is broken, he'll be upset."

"Jake is fine," the doctor says.

"He wanted to kill both of us." And then I vomit again.

"Mandy," my mother says.

"What are *you* doing here?"

"I just saw Jake. He's fine," my mother says.

"He tried to kill me, Ma. Where's Jake? Tell him he tried to kill *me*, too."

Just then, they wheel Jake's bed past my own bed.

"That's Jake over there," the doctor says. "He's going into the X-ray room."

"He's a very vain person," I say. "You'd be surprised," I say. "He tried to kill—somebody."

I come out of the delirium later that evening. Except for the fact that I'm hopelessly depressed and have suffered a medium-grade concussion, except for the fact that I am convinced that Jake has tried to kill me, my only visible injuries are two black eyes and a scratched-up chin.

"You're sure the nose isn't broken?" my mother petitions the doctor.

The doctor shakes his head.

"Sorry, Ma," I say, "maybe next time."

"You might vomit again," the doctor says. "And you have to follow the list of instructions. Remember, Mrs. Charney: Wake her up every three hours and look at the pupils. But other than vomiting and a possible head-achiness, she should be fine by tomorrow."

"I'm really depressed," I say.

"That's natural with a car accident. The adrenalin shoots way up and then—it's almost a disappointment to be alive and well. Go see Jake, dear. The police were just in there and I think he's even more depressed than you are."

I thank the doctor and start to walk out of the treatment room, but my mother lingers behind me. I know what she's thinking: As long as I'm already here, nose and all, the plastic surgery department is, after all, only two flights up. And no one would have to know. . . .

"C'mon, Ma," I say. "Not today. Not now."

"You want to see Jake?" my mother asks.

"I'm really mad at him."

"We can just go home, you know. You still feel nauseous?"

"I have a headache," I say. "I'm really mad. The whole fucking thing—you know he just *stopped* on the highway. I told the police I couldn't remember what

190

happened, but I guess there are a million witnesses anyway. What about the car?"

"I'm sure the car is a goner," my mother says. "You know, Mandy, I was just thinking . . . you have two black eyes, anyway."

"Ma, c'mon. I'll go see how Jake is doing, when they're gonna release him . . . you go wait where the soda machine is."

Just as I enter the treatment room, Chuck walks in.

"Mandy," he says. "You look great. I'm so happy!"

"Chuck, it was all his fault," I whisper. "He stopped on the highway. He's done it to me before. . . . I don't think they should let him drive."

"The police will decide all that," Chuck says. "There's no way out of this but the truth."

Together, Chuck and I approach the bed. Haven't we been through this before?

"My nose is broken," Jake says gaily. "Is the car fixable?"

"The car's totaled," Chuck says. "But never mind the car. How are *you*, champ?"

"Mandy doesn't think I'm a champ." Jake seems wildly happy.

I wonder if he's dazed from the accident. I wonder if they've given him some kind of euphoria drug. Or maybe he's finally flipped his lid entirely. It might be a relief for all of us if they just wheeled him off this second to the bonkers department. . . . Maybe he'd be happier if he was allowed to act as crazy as he wanted. He's

191

always loved to pretend he was crazy. He could go on pretending and I could go on with my life.

"Where's the 'rents?" Jake asks his brother. "Where's Mom and Dad?"

"Lucky for you, they're still not home. I don't even know where they are. They probably just went out to eat."

"You think you can convince them they never *had* a Buick?"

Chuck laughs and pats Jake's foot.

What are they so happy about? Jake is a murderer. Jake almost killed me.

"I'm kind of glad my nose is broken," Jake says then. "Now I can have whatever nose I want. Maybe I'll get a clown nose. Do they bring you a catalogue and you get to pick? Can you order a nose without koozies? Think what I'd save on tissues and nose drops."

Jake looks at me. I'm not smiling.

"Who beat you up, Mandy? Did they remove your funny bone?"

"Did they remove your brain?" I ask.

Chuck gives me a look.

"Jake, I'm going home now. I guess they'll keep you because of your nose. It *is* kind of funny, I guess. You getting a nose job. Well, I guess I better go home," I say. "I feel pretty nauseous. Did *you* have a concussion?"

"Mandy, don't talk dirty in front of my brother."

"I'll leave you two alone for a second," Chuck says sadly, and then he leaves the room.

* * *

"You tried to kill me," I say.

"I did not."

"You wish *I* was dead."

"No, I don't."

"Well, if I *was* dead, you couldn't come to the funeral. You think this is the cutest thing you ever did, but it's not . . . ."

"What *is* the cutest thing I ever did?" Jake asks slyly.

"What are you so happy about, Big Shot?"

"Little Shot," Jake says softly. "I'm Little Shot. *You're* Big Shot, remember?"

"I don't remember anything. All I remember is you tried to kill me."

"Oooh," Jake says, laughing. "What you said, sister. Oooh . . ."

"Why are you acting like a retard? What about your car? I loved that car," I say. "That was where we did it—the second time. Remember?"

"We'll get another car," he says. "We'll do it again and again."

"Are you tired of trying to kill yourself? You think you're finally bored with trying to kill people?"

"Now that you mention it," Jake says brightly, "now that you mention it, I'm happy to be alive."

"Really?" I ask.

"Yes."

I soften. "Well, if you're *really* happy now, then maybe it was all worth it. Give me back some money, then. I can't afford to keep paying you the dollar a day to stay alive."

"No," Jake says. "I'm saving that money to buy you a wedding surprise. I have thirty-three dollars of yours."

"I've given you thirty-three dollars? You're kidding."

"Uh-uh."

"Then give me some of it back to buy steaks with. I need some big expensive steaks to put on my shiners."

"I love your shiners," Jake says. "Kiss me."

"I can't kiss you. Your nose is broken. Doesn't it hurt?"

"Leetle," he says. "They shot me up with something. I haven't been this high since second grade."

"Well, I still love you," I say. "And whatever they shot you up with does wonders for your personality. It's nice to see you happy," I say.

"What did you tell the pigs?" Jake asks.

"That I couldn't remember anything. But it doesn't matter what *I* said. Two million people saw you stop on the highway. And Chuck says we have to tell the cops the truth. Why, what did *you* tell them?"

"I told them you were driving," he says. "I said it was all *your* fault."

"Okay, buddy. Keep up the good work. Blame it all on me. I don't mind. I don't have a personality. Make doody on me, do whatever you want."

"Don't talk dirty, Mandy. After the nose job, we'll have an unveiling. We'll invite all the relatives. The *machetaynestes*," Jake says.

"Even Mimi Greenwald?" I ask.

"If she does a striptease, she can come."

"I'll get in touch with her agent," I say. "I better go. My mother's waiting. My mother wants *me* to get a nose job. She's probably pissed your nose is broken instead of mine. Call me tonight and tell me what the story is. I'll come down here tomorrow if my parents let me. In the meantime, try to get your regular nose back."

194

"Never," Jake says. "I'm gonna get a nose like Harpo. This is my chance to look like a star."

"You are a star," I say. "I love you," I say.

"I love you, baby. You aren't mad, are you?"

"No," I say. "I'll see you—in court."

Outside the treatment room, Chuck is sneakily crying.

"Chuck," I say. "What is it?"

"Nothing," he says nasally. "How is he, you think?"

"He sounds better than he's sounded in weeks. What did they give him?"

"I think they gave him a really strong mood elevator. Nold was in here before. Jake told the doctors to get him. He wouldn't talk to anyone else."

"Nold was here? Jake didn't even tell me. No wonder he seemed so happy. Nold shot him up. So what did he say—finally?"

"He says he's in pretty bad shape. The fact that he tried to kill both of you might mean he's pretty serious. Nold thinks he's gonna succeed one of these times. Three times in six weeks. It sounds lousy to me. Lousy."

"You're afraid now, aren't you?"

"I'm terrified," Chuck says.

"Don't be terrified," I say. Mandy is a mother.

"Aren't you?" he asks.

"Terrified? No. It's like I've almost—accepted it."

"You've been through a lot, haven't you? I'm sorry, Mandy. I didn't realize. This thing is definitely getting out of hand. But don't *accept* what he's doing. Don't give up. He needs *you* more than anybody. Oh, this is so depressing. . . . I think maybe we better *all* go see the psychiatrist. Together. I can't—can I?—ask you to just hang in there—for us?"

I am almost grown up.

"Listen, Chuck, I feel like something's different now. Like Jake has maybe gotten it out of his system. Like maybe now he's seen that he *is* effective—I mean they say that suicide comes from a sense of your own unimportance. Like you want to kill yourself to show people—"

"Mandy, the intellectual stuff doesn't work. When Jake first did it, that first time, you know, I started reading Durkheim, all that technical crap. But it *is* crap, Mandy. There's a kid in there *dying*. My brother is dying and Anne Sexton poetry doesn't help."

"I didn't know you read Anne Sexton! I love Anne Sexton," I say brightly.

"Mandy, help me. Help us save him. I know it's a terrible thing to ask. But I beg of you, Mandy. We need you. And don't forget how much *you* need Jake."

Do I need Jake?

"Chuck, I can't handle this. I feel so weird. *My life* passed before me today. It really happens like that. Life is so incredibly fragile. . . ."

Standing there in the corridor of Bellevue Hospital, I am feeling otherworldly. I feel the pain start to ease up, releasing itself slowly. Bubbling out of my bowels, effervescing up through my veins to the air where it oxidizes, transforms. The pain is not pain anymore. I have made some kind of deal with the devil. In exchange for a moment of release from pain, I have given the devil everything: the hottest and purest of my moments with Jake, the flotsam of puppy love, the kitty litter, the stuffing, of all my days as a child. I have

196

traded away not my love for Jake, but rather the belief in this love. No longer do I breathe so hurtfully, because love itself no longer hurts. Or so I think, one day in my life.

"What do you say, Mandy?"

"I never meant I would walk away. You misunderstood what I meant. I meant we'd never get married. I finally realize it's all a scam. . . ."

"It's not a scam, Mandy."

"Of course it is," I say. "I think I've finally stopped loving him romantically. I think I wouldn't even get *jealous* anymore. I love him different now. As a friend."

"That makes me sad," Chuck says.

"That's because you're a romantic. And your brother is the biggest romantic who ever lived. And he's fucking *dying* of romanticism. He can't grow up. He won't accept things moving on."

"But, Mandy, *you're* romanticizing. *You're* being intellectual. What we have to be now is *practical*."

"Marriage is practical," I say. "Loony bins are also practical."

"You sound like you've got *hard* or something," Chuck says, pained. "I guess you're just growing up. But Jake is still like a kid."

"He *is* a kid," I say. "But he's also a man. And that's what he has to realize. He has no sense at all of his power. He's a *very* powerful person, you know. Every girl falls in love with him."

"Is that what power is?" Chuck laughs.

"I mean he has magnetism. Almost scary magnetism. I think people would listen to him, do what he wants.

He could be a guru or something. Or a Charles Manson, even. If he was bad or crazy, I mean."

I've said the wrong thing. I've said lots of wrong things, but there's no going back now. From now on I'm Queen Practical. I'll do what I can to help him, but I'm not going down with his ship.

No matter how beautiful is that ship, or lovely, I won't go down. Jake's ship is a perfect craft: Its cargo is babies, its cargo is light. Jake's ship is a mighty boat which breaks through waters cleanly, dolls' teacup parties trembling in its wake. The foam is the same green-blue as my eyes, the water smells heavenly as Christ's water sac, the waters part good-naturedly to let his baby-blue tugboat trudge by.

The *S.S. Jacob* is a sweet-hearted ship, its cargo is babies, it runs on a fuel that orphan girls mix from nectar and yawns. It's a seaworthy ship, a heartworthy ship, the purest transport in any town. But I spot the leak under the bow, I see the patch job at starboard can't hold. I take my two nostrils into my hand and I hold my nose severely and jump. Mandy the diehard has deserted ship. Watch Mandy swim for shore and her life.

"Listen, Chuck. I'm really sorry I said those things— about Charles Manson. I didn't mean to say *that*. It's just that I've had a crazy day. And I *did* have a concussion. So don't even listen to me. Nothing's changed," I lie. "I'm still going to do whatever I can for Jake and I'll *try* not to be so down. . . ."

198

"I'll be in touch," Chuck says.

"My mother," I say. He nods. I walk out.

"I had a really strange talk with Chuck," I tell my mother, riding shotgun in the car.

"Don't you have to go back and register, Mandy?"

"I think I'll just call the Dean and try to get out of school for a while. No one knows what's going on, anyway. You know these hippie schools."

"So now Sarah Lawrence is a *hippie* school?" My mother raises thin eyebrows.

"Well, not an astrology–basket-weaving school, but you know—unstructured, independent. You're *supposed* to miss school because your boyfriend's dying. Then you write it all up and get credit for Sociology."

"My, we're getting cynical," my mother says. "Are you growing a new personality? Don't get tough, Mandy. I hate tough young girls."

"Me, tough?" I laugh. "And I don't feel so young, Ma. This business with Jake is exhausting. I feel like an old lady."

"This summer *has* been terrible, hasn't it? And I still can't get over it. *He* gets the broken nose. A nose like Tyrone Power's, and he gets the broken nose."

"That's life," my new personality says.

"He gets the broken nose all right. And you get the broken heart."

"Mandy," Mrs. Rinehart says, over telephone wires. "Mandy, Chuck says you're fine."

"I *am* fine," I say, "more or less. I only have a concussion and two black eyes."

"That's all?" she says. "What else do you *need*?"

"Are you angry about the car?"

"How can I be angry about a car? As long as you two are safe. And, thank God, I just found out, no one in the other car was hurt."

"Did the Big Shot have his nose fixed?"

"They set it early this evening. He made me so crazy, too, with his *mishegoss*. I was ready to kill him. He wanted the doctor to give him a funny nose. He kept *insisting*. I really think he would have done it, too, if I wasn't there. Imagine!"

"Well, at least *you* sound all right. I had a long conversation with Chuck. He thinks we should all go see Nold. Together. Maybe it's an idea," I say.

"Whatever Chuck thinks is right. Are you going back to school?"

"Uh-uh. I can't see the point now. All I can think about is Jake—I'd like to see things settled—or something."

"Are you two going to get married?" Her voice sounds urgent now. Does she want me to marry him now, or what? From her voice it's impossible to tell. But she's scared all right. She's scared, Chuck's scared, they're all scared, these *machetaynestes*. But don't they know I can't save him? That love can't save him? That I'm only extra weight on a sagging, bottom-going ship?

"Marriage seems like a bad idea now."

"But maybe it would—" Her voice breaks cleanly. She's crying. "I'm sorry, Mandy. I can't tell you what to do."

"We *can't* get married," I say. "We're too young. Aren't we too young?" I ask.

"God only knows," she says.

"I guess I want to be too young. I can't even imagine getting married. . . ."

"You've got to do what you want in this world." Her voice grows distant now, floats away from my ear.

Downstairs, a friend is at the door.

"Mandy, there's someone here to see you!"

Is the friend a real friend? Twenty years old, I am unsure if I have real friends.

"Mandy, this is Fred." My best friend from high school hands me her six-month-old baby. The baby is wearing a vagabond diaper made from an old dish towel. Bonnie and I start laughing.

"At least your baby's a hippie," I say.

"Oh, you," she says, kissing me awkwardly on the cheek. "Your face is broken out," she says.

"I'm always broken out. Where'd *you* come from?"

"Outer space," Bonnie says, and laughs. In her laugh sounds the same clumsy love-hate Bonnie has always felt towards everything: me; herself; her husband, Joe; honors history; politics; sex.

Bonnie and I were passionate friends at sixteen and seventeen and eighteen. We fought all the time, called each other terrible names, told each other the brutal truth before it became *de rigueur*. We spent three terrible years smoking pot underneath her mother's baby grand, gobbling whole bags of peanut clusters, tipping the scales in gleeful defiance of Twiggy, Mary Quant, and The Shrimp. And all the while cutting classes in our racially unrested high school where Black girls spit Yankee pot roast at us, brazen hippie chicks, for not wearing brassieres.

"Oh, Bonnie! Why didn't you ever write to me?"

"I felt stupid being married."

"You're *embarrassed* to be married?"

"I'm getting so straight," she says.

"Did you get pregnant first or married first?"

"I've been married two years," she says. "The baby's only six months."

"Why didn't you even invite me to the wedding?"

"We didn't have a real wedding. And you know our relationship was always peculiar."

"Yours and mine? Or yours and Joe's?"

"Both," she says.

"Where *is* Joe?"

"In Texas."

"Doing what?"

"Doing a thing with some arts-and-crafts person. She makes feather halters for department stores. But she's not so bad. I tripped with her once and we talked about Joe and stuff. It's okay, Mandy. It's not what you think."

"What do I think?"

"That I'm Sadie Married Lady and I'm all abandoned."

"But Joe never seemed the type. . . ."

"You sound like my parents. Listen—I want him to do what he wants and I want to do what I want. And it doesn't *depress* me."

"It can't make you feel good."

202

"The baby is hungry," she says, hoisting up her shirt.

"How can you tell? Doesn't he *cry* when he's hungry?"

"Not usually. We're very plugged into each other's needs. I can tell when he's hungry and maybe he can tell when my nerves can't handle him crying."

"That's great," I say.

"Can you believe my tits?" she asks.

"They were always intense," I say.

"Yeah, but now I'm *really* a cow."

"You don't look cowy. You look like Sophia Loren." She laughs.

"You have to show Fred to my parents."

"Where'd you get your black eyes?"

"How come you just noticed them now?"

"I don't know."

"You tell me I have pimples, but ignore two black eyes. And my chin. Do I look horrible?"

"You look like Cloris Leachman," she says.

"You get to be Sophia Loren and I get to be Cloris Leachman?"

"I *like* Cloris Leachman," she says. "So who beat you up? A man?"

"What else?" I say. "No, nothing that serious. Jake just tried to kill me, that's all. On the highway. He stopped the car in the middle of the road."

"You're *still* seeing *him*?"

"Constantly."

"When did he start being nice to you?"

"After I had an abortion. I mean, I didn't even lay it on him. I didn't even tell him actually, till he kind of made me. Then something came over him. He started feeling *responsible*. . . ."

"He was *never* responsible. He was meaner to you than Joe ever was to me. I mean it. And Joe is no prize as far as *responsible* either."

"It's different. You're *married*."

"*Married*—it's a joke. It's not like we know *why* we're married. And he's pretty immature. In high school, I always thought he was this really *mature* person. He shaved his head in twelfth grade, so *I* thought he was mature. He isn't mature—he's an old man. He gets me *so* down."

"Why do you let him have other relationships?"

"I don't like to *press*ure people. And I don't *feel* like a masochist. Do I *seem* like a masochist to you?"

"Don't ask *me*. I'm the one with the black eyes. Jake really tried to *kill* me."

"Just because he stopped on the highway doesn't mean he tried to *kill* you. That's melodramatic, Mandy."

"I've *always* been melodramatic."

"Yeah. But I can't believe you're still *seeing* him. You know, I never even knew him in high school. Before he got kicked out, he used to sell nickel bags during homeroom. Nickel bags—can you believe it? But I never really saw you together. I always kind of thought you were—well, not making him up, but—you know—"

"Embellishing?"

"Yeah."

"I really loved him, Bonnie. I've loved him since I was eleven. . . ."

"But in all the time we were friends, you had maybe three dates."

"Not *three*. But that's when he used to ignore me. I'm still not sure *why* he ignored me. I used to think I

204

wasn't cool enough. But maybe he just didn't want me to know what a big hippie he was. He always used to make fun of hippies and people who smoked pot."

"In the meantime, he's *selling* pot during homeroom. What a hypocrite."

"He wanted me to think he was pure. He always had this weird kind of *purity* thing."

"So have you, Mandy."

"I guess . . ."

"But probably it's just that you're always feeling *guilty*. Which is why I'm trying not to hassle Joe about that feather woman in Texas. We were all raised on guilt. And I don't want Fred to have to deal with all that crap—"

"Fred, where'd you get that name?"

"You think it's funny, don't you? Everybody thinks it's funny. I picked it because—don't laugh—it's real. I want him to be a realist. Look at us—Bonita and Amanda. Who were they trying to kid?"

"Like we're society girls or something."

"Like we're not Jewish, you mean."

"You're right, I guess."

"What are you going to *do*, Mandy? About Jake, I mean. Why did he try to fuck up the car?"

"He's trying to kill himself. This is the third time."

"Does he always waste cars?"

"No, the car's a new development. Twice he took pills and tried to O.D."

"What kind of pills?" Bonnie asks solemnly, trying not to smile, affecting clinical disinterest.

"Triavane? Something like that. Some kind of mood elevator."

"Oh yeah?" she says. "Like Ritalin, I bet. Can you get me some?"

"They don't get you high," I say. "They have to build up in your blood system."

"No *they* don't. *Everything* gets you high. If you take enough."

"I'm not going to encourage you. They're prescription, and besides, you're nursing."

"Yeah," she says, faraway. "I was into some weird things, you know. Before Fred was born. I was doing smack for a while with Joe. In Tucson," she says dreamily.

"Really?" I ask.

"Yes, Mandy, *really*. You're such a baby Girl Scout," she says.

"Am I *still*? I thought I was becoming mildly groovy."

"You'll *never* be groovy," she says playfully, unhooking her baby from her nipple. The nipple is as brown as gravy, as large as a little toe, a snout.

"Freddy is sleeping," she says.

"We can put him on the bed here," I say, smoothing out the bedspread.

"You have a box—like a carton or something? I can put him in a carton and bring him down to your mother. Maybe she'll watch him for a while and we can get high."

"Sure," I say, laughing. And we take the stairs together, arm in friend's arm.

"Mandy, it's *your* turn to say something funny." Jake has called from the hospital.

"I heard you really tried to get your nose done funny. Your mother couldn't believe it."

"Yeah, she made the doctor just *mush* it back together. Say something *funny*, Mandy. I'm really depressed. And my parents weren't even pissed about the car."

"That's because you're spoiled rotten."

"I loved that car—like a brother."

"They'll buy you another car."

"You think I'm spoiled."

"You *are* spoiled, Jake."

"You think I'm doing this shit for attention?"

"Are you?" I ask.

"Who knows?"

"You *have to* know. It's your life."

"No one knows what they're doing," Jake says. "At least I know that much. You think *you* know what *you're* doing?"

"Sometimes," I say. "But I'm not like you," I say. "You're a genius."

In my voice there is a slippery irony Jake doesn't pick up on.

"I *am* a genius," he says. "And I *am* going to be famous."

"Bonnie is over here. It's been three years."

"Bonnie Jacobson? She's a cute girl."

"You used to sell her pot in homeroom. I never even knew that."

"I only did it like twice. It was Leonard's idea."

"And you used to act like I was a junkie for smoking it. Boy, Jake, you can really be full of shit sometimes."

"Did you know if you get constipated in the hospital the doctor takes it all out with his hands?"

"Why are you telling me that?"

" 'Cause you said I was full of shit."

"I take it back," I say.

"That's better."

"I said you used to be full of shit."

Bonnie picks up her carton and laughs her soft, bitter laugh. "So I'm going back to Austin tomorrow to re-claim my old man," she says.

"A good idea," I say.

"My mother wants me to stay awhile. But a week in Bel Ridge is all I can handle."

"I can relate to that. I've been here all summer and now I don't even know when I'll be going back to school. I'm kind of waiting for Jake to get it to-gether. . . ."

"Decide if he wants to kill himself or not?"

"I don't know. He's tried to kill himself three times. He could go on like this forever."

"Don't let him manipulate you. Go back to school. *Do* something. You can't just hang out here waiting for him to make up his mind."

"But every time I try to do something, he manipu-lates me back into this suicide thing. . . ."

"Some people—men especially—need a lot of atten-tion. And they'll take your last little bit of energy—"

"I know it sounds—paranoid—but I think he's trying to sabotage me. On purpose, I mean."

"I believe you. Don't let him."

"I don't even know if I want to marry him anymore."

"Don't get married," Bonnie says. "Whatever you do, don't get married and don't get pregnant either."

"Then what should I get?"

"Get rich," she says. "Get smart. Get laid. Take care, old friend," she says softly.

Chuck invites me to a group meeting with the psychiatrist. First we go out to breakfast—Mr. and Mrs. Rinehart, Chuck and Sandy, me and Jake—first we go out for breakfast at Sid and Syl's Deli, and then on to Manhattan to confront Dr. Nold.

"Why is Sandy going?" my mother asks.

"I know," I say. "It *is* strange, isn't it?"

"It sounds like a party," she says.

"It's the new thing in psychiatry. Group confrontation. I'm sure it *will* be a scream. Too bad *you* can't come. Then it *really* would be funny. I wonder if Mimi Greenwald should come, too. Jake has this weird fixation on her."

"And Jake gets to confront her and tell her she wears too much makeup?"

"Something like that."

"And then he tells his parents how much he resents them?"

"I don't even think he *does* resent his parents."

"Everyone resents his parents. It's natural."

"Do you think I resent you?" I ask.

"Don't you?" she says. "Children always remember only the bad."

"I don't remember anything bad."

"A dress I wouldn't buy you?"

"Oh sure—there's always that kind of thing if you want to dig it all up."

"I remember having to wear boys' shoes during the Depression. Brown suede bucks."

"Do you resent Nana and Grandpa?"

"No," she says. "I don't want to. I don't like to remember unpleasant things."

"See?"

And then, perversely, my mind fills up with all kinds of shoddy cargo: Mary Janes with taps hammered on instead of regulation tap shoes, a vinyl waist cincher when everyone had leather. I try to will these images away, to remember, instead, the good. A baby bracelet in sixth grade with *blue* beads instead of pink.

Outside, the Rineharts' Mercedes honks three times.

"Have fun," my mother says gaily. But her voice comes to me from far away. She is back in the thirties and kids are throwing mud pies, now dog pies, at her brown suede bucks.

"You get in the back with Jake and Sandy. Chuck, you come up here."

"Maybe Mandy wants to sit in the front."

"We could take two cars," Jake says.

"We only *have* one car now."

"Let's rent a car," Jake says, "until the new one comes. Let's rent an XKE and I'll drive it," Jake says.

* * *

"There's Bobby Archiello." I nudge Jake as Manny maneuvers the car into the lot.

"I'm getting down," Jake says, arranging his body across the hump of the back-seat floor.

"What are you doing?" Annette asks. "You used to be *friends* with Bobby. You never see any of your friends anymore."

"I'm not getting out of this car," Jake says, "until that cat leaves the parking lot."

"Do you owe him money, or what?" Chuck asks, laughing at his brother, who is spread out full length across the floor of the car.

"Well, I think this is nonsense," Annette Rinehart says. "And I'm going in. You can stay here and starve."

Annette and Manny walk up the steps of the diner. Sandy stands in the middle of the lot, admiring a pink Renault. Chuck and I stand on either side of the car, shaking our heads at Jake, who has now put a paper bag over his head.

"Don't say my name—either of you. I'll just wear this bag over my head and Archiello won't know who I am."

"Yes he will, Jake. Especially if he sees *me*. Jake, he's looking right at me—now. I have to wave—do something—Jake!"

"Just don't say my name. Call me Rufus."

Jake gets out of the car, then, and Sandy starts laughing. Across the bag is printed an advertisement for a local lingerie store. Jake's nose puffs out strategically against a line drawing of a woman in bra and panty girdle.

"Hey Jacob! How ya' doin'?" Bobby Archiello slips the bag easily from over Rufus Rinehart's head.

* * *

Manny Rinehart is having the Kishke Surprise. "I don't know why they call it 'Surprise,'" he confides to me. "After you've had it once, you always know what's in it," he says.

Annette smiles at Manny. "And what are you kids having?" she asks.

"I want the Fisherman's Catch," Jake whines like a baby boy.

"It's *breakfast*," Annette says. "You don't want all that fried fish for breakfast."

"Yes, I do. I'm hungry," Jake says.

"You don't *look* hungry," his mother says. "You look like you should go on a diet."

Lately Jake has been putting on weight. He's only five five, but he must weigh 160. Jake looks forlorn.

"I'm fat and I'm bald," Jake says.

"If you think *you're* bald, look at me," Chuck says. "Or look at Dad."

"But you both have wives. And jobs."

"I love a bald man," Sandy coos, stroking Chuck's bald spot.

"Quit it, San. I'm not exactly Yul Brynner," Chuck sighs, shaking off Sandy's hand. Sandy strokes the spot again, purring.

"Quit it, Sandy. Or I'll tell everybody what you did last night."

"What did she do?" Jake asks.

"Well, last night we were getting ready for—" Sandy clamps her hand over her husband's mouth, but Chuck struggles free. "Last night . . ."

"I'll kill you. I'll divorce you," Sandy says.

"Don't tell," Annette says. "Married people have a right not to tell."

"Tell, tell," Jake says. "We're all *machetaynestes*."

"Well," Chuck begins. He looks across the booth at Sandy, and then he stops. Sandy is crying. "Don't be mad, Sandy. I wasn't really going to tell."

"Yes, you were," she says, pushing away her place mat, pushing her fork and spoon and knife. She teeters her coffee cup and mine and heads for the bathroom.

"Sandy gets so moody," Chuck says. "Maybe *she* needs to go back to Nold."

"I didn't know Sandy went to Nold," Jake says.

"See? You're not the only one with problems." Annette pats her son's hand. "It's her mother, isn't it? Her mother makes her neurotic."

"The Vulture," Jake joins in. "No wonder."

"Forget it, all of you," Chuck says. "Mandy, Mom, someone go in there and tell her I was only fooling."

"I'll go," I say bravely as the waitress approaches the table.

"And who gets the Fisherman's Catch?" she asks. "And which lucky boy or girl gets the Kishke Surprise?"

In the bathroom, Sandy is curling her lashes. We always seem to talk in bathrooms, Sandy and I.

"Why does he always have to make our marriage into a comedy act?" she says.

"He was only kidding. He wasn't really going to tell."

"Oh yes he was. He loves making me look ridiculous in front of his family."

"You don't look ridiculous," I say. "You look like Shirley MacLaine."

"*Shirley* MacLaine? You *think* so? I love Shirley MacLaine."

Heading back to our table, Sandy nudges me. "That's *him*," she whispers. "Dr. Nold—over there. He's sitting at our table."

"I didn't know he lived on the Island," I say to Sandy.

"Ssshh," she nudges me, as we start to sit down.

"I'll sit on the aisle," I say. "I don't mind." The doctor doesn't mind either. He has taken over my window seat and seems to be enjoying his meal immensely. I watch him dip a whole *bialy* into *my* coffee cup as the waitress pulls over an extra chair for me on the aisle.

"This is Mandy Charney, Jake's sweetheart," Annette says brightly.

The doctor waves his roll at me.

"What do you think of Jake?" Annette asks the doctor. "Don't you think he's putting on a little too much weight?"

"Later, we'll get down to business," the doctor says, smearing a second *bialy* with vegetable-flecked cream cheese. "Their *bialys* get worse every year." The doctor looks to Manny for confirmation. "In all the years I've been coming here, the baked goods just keep deteriorating."

"I know what you mean, Doctor." Manny smiles sagely. "It used to be a bagel here was really a bagel.

214

Now," he says, "they're like packaged. Aren't they, Annette?"

"So, Doctor," Manny says in the parking lot. "Not that we really have much room—but we're going to your office anyway. Maybe you'd like a lift?"

"I have my car," the doctor says, pointing out a Renault the color of belly lox.

"What did you think?" Annette jokes. "He came with a helicopter?"

In the back seat of the car, Jake looks at me, his eyes rolling wildly. "Only in my life do these things happen. Only in my crazy life."

"And how are you, Sandra?" Dr. Nold says as the six of us find seats in the doctor's dining room.

"I heard—about your wife," Sandy says, "and I'm really sorry."

The psychiatrist clears his throat. He is short, paunchy, a brand-new widower with thick glasses and a lot of hair. Earlier, on the car ride in, Jake assured me his hair is really a rug, a piece.

"But what about *you*, Sandra? How is life treating you these days?"

"Maybe I should make an appointment," Sandy giggles nervously. "I don't feel like talking about it—now."

"We're all here to help each other," Dr. Nold says. "Since you chose to come along, Sandra, we expect you to be open about your feelings. If everyone is open and honest, maybe we can all help each other a little bit."

"All right. I hate my husband," Sandy says.

"You *hate* your husband?" Annette says, shocked. "No, you don't."

"How could anyone hate Chuckie?" Manny asks. "He works so hard to make a nice home for you and the baby."

"He works hard all right," Sandy says. "All day and all night. He's probably having—"

"What? Having what, Sandy?" Chuck butts in.

"Having a great time eating lunches and showing off to everybody what a big intellectual he is. He *quotes* Thomas Jefferson at me when I'm trying to sleep. And all I get to do is *kak* around that depressing apartment. . . ."

"Depressing?" Chuck says. "What's so depressing all of a sudden about toil de Jewie?"

"*Toile de Jouy*," Sandy says sadly. "You can't even pronounce things right. I don't know why I married you. And I don't know why we have to live in Brooklyn. Nobody lives in Brooklyn."

"Nobody lives in Brooklyn?" Chuck says. Barbra Streisand lived in Brooklyn. Hart Crane *immortalized* Brooklyn. Judge Samuel Leibowitz lived in Brooklyn."

"I'm sick of sitting in Brooklyn watching my nails grow."

"Listen, you ungrateful—"

"Enough!" Annette Rinehart clamps her hands over her ears. "I can't stand this fighting. I always thought you two got along like a couple of lovebirds."

"There's no reason to get upset, Mrs. Rinehart. I realize this all seems a bit unusual to you—Sandra and

Chuck showing their anger like this in front of all of us. But I assure you, yelling is a positive expression of true feelings. Now, I want you to trust me with this— Can you trust me, Mrs. Rinehart?"

"Trust him, Annette," Manny chuckles. "It's sixty dollars an hour."

"I trust, I trust," Annette says, looking at Manny, bewildered.

Jake lights up a cigar.

"Jake," the psychiatrist says. "Must you smoke that thing now?"

"He wants attention," I say. I want to show Dr. Nold how perceptive I am.

"Do *you* want attention?" the psychiatrist asks. "What's on your mind, Mandy?"

"About Chuck and Sandy's fight?"

"Whatever's on your mind."

"I think Jake should promise us all he won't kill himself. But what I was thinking about before was—I was thinking about you know how you always wish you'd ordered something else—in a restaurant? I wish I'd—"

"Let's all go around in a circle and tell Jake how we're feeling. Can we try that—just as an exercise?" The psychiatrist looks into my eyes. "I'll go first," he says. "Jake, I'm angry with you for not keeping your contract. . . ."

"Contract?" Manny asks. "What contract? Did you sign anything?"

"So, you think it really accomplished something?" Annette looks at Manny. Manny's smile is dreamlike and his hands hold the wheel at ten past ten.

And I, sitting between them, turn my head around to look at Jake. But Jake is not looking at me. He is watching Chuck and Sandy, who are speaking goo-goo talk and nuzzling in each other's hair.

Jake and I lie upstairs in his room with the door locked. He is playing a tape of an old Symphony Sid program. The show was aired exactly, he tells me, one October ago.

"It *was* smart of me to tape these shows, wasn't it? You always laugh at me for taping everything, but now you see why. Now I can still listen to Sid. It's like he's still on the air. Imagine if I had tapes of everything? My grandfather— Wouldn't it be great if I could turn on the machine and listen to my grandpa?"

"That *would* be nice, baby," I say, adjusting my position, snuggling in as close as possible to his masculine chest. I turn towards his face to kiss him, and feel, before I see, his tears.

"I thought you were happy, honey."

"I *am* happy," he says.

"Are you crying because of your grandfather?"

"No, yes. I don't know. Let's make a tape of us."

"What kind of tape? Whenever you want me to be funny, I can't."

"Not a funny tape, a nice one. I'll turn the machine on and you just say nice things about me and I'll tell you how beautiful you are."

"We don't need the machine," I say. "We can do it without the machine."

"No," he says seriously. "I want it all on tape. To remember."

218

"We don't have to remember that way. We have years and years to say nice things to each other. Just like Chuck and Sandy," I say. "Were you upset today? By the stuff we all said to you? I was really embarrassed when I said that thing about the restaurant. I could tell Nold doesn't like me. . . ."

"Everybody likes you, Mandy. And actually the whole thing turned out to be a scream. I never realized Chuck and Sandy got on each other's nerves so much. I think it upset my mother, though."

"They *did* get a little vicious. I didn't think they talked that way either. I thought they had this ideal setup. But I guess no marriage is ideal. And maybe they were kind of showing off anyway—trying to shock your parents."

"When we get married, it won't be like that, will it?" Jake looks at me.

"Who knows? We fight, too. Everybody fights."

"But we'll be different, right, Mand?"

"We *are* different," I say sadly. "Sometimes I wish we weren't so different."

"Why? You want us to fight? About furniture? And money?"

"That's not what I meant. I meant—"

Jake kisses me then. He sucks in all of my breath. The kiss is like a seltzer, a Tums. It takes all the pain away.

"I know what you meant," he says. "Don't worry." And then he kisses me.

V

J AKE DECIDES TO MOVE OUT of his family's house. He does finally manage to register at N.Y.U. film school, but the semester is already three weeks old by the time his registration cards wend their way underneath the university seal. He calls me up at Sarah Lawrence to tell me he hates his courses.

"I don't like any of the teachers," he says. "They don't even *talk* about my favorite movies. And they don't have *one* course on Irving Pichel."

"Who's Irving Pichel?"

"*Life Begins at Eight-Thirty*, Mandy. *Destination Moon. The Sheik Steps Out.* He *directed* all the movies I love. I took you to *see Destination* two times. I even paid for you the first time."

"Well, maybe later, when you've been there a while, you can find somebody who'll talk to you about the old movies. You just *started*, Jake."

"Yeah, well it ain't any fun. How can *you* stand school, Mandy?"

"You know I always liked it, Jake. I was always good at academics. Teachers like me."

"You're the first person I ever *talked to* who got all A's. No one could believe it—Leonard still can't understand why a smart girl would go out with me."

"Leonard's only kidding. Leonard thinks you're a genius, too. How *is* Leonard anyway? Does he write to you?"

"He sent me a fishhook. I still don't understand what the joke is. He hates film school, too. But at least he gets to go swimming and play in the sand with girls."

"I'll play in the sand with you."

"Mandy, I'm really depressed. About school. And I'm probably dropping out soon. So don't be surprised."

"Did you tell your parents?"

"No. But I guess I better tell them. I feel like I should at least finish off the semester. They paid two thousand dollars and I already missed the first three weeks."

"The money isn't what bothers them, Jake. They want you to *be* something, have a career."

"I have a career. I can play at the Mandala any night I want. Even without Leonard."

"But Jake, they don't pay you."

"Fox said he'd start giving me fifteen a night—and beer—after Christmas."

"You *spend* more than fifteen a night on records and everything."

"I'm getting the apartment, though. I decided I can't live at home."

"Why not? Your parents leave you alone."

"They said they'd pay for an apartment the first six months. By then I could get something going—some comedy on my own. Or maybe I could hook up with a girl singer. A beautiful Black chick. I always wanted a Black girl to sing with."

"Thanks a lot."

"To sing with," I said.

"Hire *me*, Jake."

"You can't *sing*, Mandy."

"You love it when I sing. . . ."

"Well, listen, Mandy. This call is on Dorothy K. and I have to get a new number. I think this one isn't good anymore. The operator sounded suspicious. I better get off."

"All right," I say. "Try to stay in school a while longer. Try to at least finish the semester."

"I don't think I can, Mandy. But to get them to pay for the apartment, maybe I'll pretend I'm still going."

"Why can't you just *make* yourself go?"

"I can't do it, Mandy. It really depresses me. The girls at N.Y.U. are horrible. They keep coming up to me and asking, 'You Jewish?' "

"Well you're not looking for girls anyway. Are you, Jake?"

"I'm looking for you," he says.

"I'm right here, baby. I'm always right here."

"One more thing," Jake says. "We have to go to this horrible party. In about two weeks. The Vulture is having a party for Sandy's brother. He's getting engaged or something. Remember Leon? The one with the funny eyebrows?"

"He was at Sandy's surprise party, wasn't he?"

"I guess. I don't want to go. It's going to be really fancy. My mother says I have to go. So you have to, too."

"I don't mind going," I say. "I'm dying to see her apart—"

The operator cuts in then. "This is the operator," she says. "May I ask who you were just speaking with?" I hang up the hall phone quickly, but the operator rings back.

"Are you the party who was just on the phone?"

"This is a dormitory, a college. God knows who used the phone last."

"*I* know," she says sharply. We don't need God to arrest people."

Back at college, I want to have fun. The summer has been no fun at all. June and July I worked in an office above a head shop, soliciting money for Mental Health, calling up doctors and T.V. repairmen, asking them to buy tickets in order that a schizzy little boy or girl might spend a sane-making day at the circus: "I'm calling for Nassau County Mental Health. Would you like to buy a retard?"

And then, as the summer wore on into August, Jake began to take up my time. To take it up painfully, accusingly, paranoiacally. And then the disillusionment of the writers' conference: a lesson in bullyhood and violence, lessons in gratuitous pain, lessons in the hollowness of power and fame—the difficulty of dreams you never meant to come true.

All of these lessons in life leave me sad, frustrated, lonely, alone. Perhaps I am finally beginning to see Jake's side.

Before, I *wanted* to grow up, to pay rent on my own

apartment, to sleep with a husband instead of a boy, to name and nurse and nudge my own babies into the thick folds of life. A credit rating, a legal diaphragm, monogrammed towels, a master bedroom. And now I want to be a child, to not have anything count.

Ever since elementary school, they've been talking to us about growing up, waving our records in our faces, wagging Manila folders so threateningly, some of us— Jake—decided even then, mere children, we wanted out.

But me? I never wanted out. I was one of the tractable kids, the good girl who joined library council, not so it would look good on her record, but because she wanted to be a good citizen, responsible, effectual, a do-gooder. And now? I don't want a record. I want a small green slate, the squeaky blackboard of childhood, a slate you can keep erasing.

In eighth grade, I ran for recording secretary. I "hired" a popular girl, a good girl, to be my campaign manager. Four feet nine with my loafers on, I trembled up there on the stage while another good girl, a popular girl, belted my campaign song to the tune of "The Girl from Ipanema," the lyrics composed by a good boy, grooming himself even at fifteen for hot footlights and fevered discussion of his latest Broadway revue.

In the nether rows of Daniel Webster Junior High School, the rows where the bad boys and cutups sat, there sat Jake secretly reading *The Best of Marvel Comics*, unconscious of my bony knees knocking wildly under the podium, unconscious of my love for him, a bad boy with a bad record.

While Carolee Gass stood selling the lyrics, Jake Rinehart picked his Tyrone Power nose, sticking the bonus of his efforts onto the music teacher's sweater, the exploits of the Incredible Hulk fanning out across less nervous knees.

> *Smart and punctual, young and stunning,*
> *Mandy Charney for recording secretary*
>   *is running . . .*
> *And if you select her,*
> *Why then, you'll elect her, you know. . . .*

How could bad-boy Jake have known the good girl on the stage was his girl? And how could he—or I—have known I belonged there in the back with him, pasting koozies to Mrs. Freibisch's back?

Suddenly, in my junior year of college, my childhood seems a brutal deception. I'd been betrayed by the years of training, by guidance counselors and the *P.T.A. News.* Why hadn't anyone told me the good girl doesn't always win? Maybe my father had tried to warn me, cynical and ironic was his influence even then. But he'd been a bad-boy cutup himself, had done his own time in the back rows, probably wondered, wise as he was, if neat penmanship and good behavior might not, in the end, be the way.

But now, sprawled out on the college-service linen good girls get to sleep on, I realize I've been had. Your elementary school record turns into your credit rating, your credit rating turns into the furniture you never really own. By the time the last installment is paid, the loveseat yields no more love, the easy chair feels difficult, the draperies look like *dreck*.

As much as I try to study, I can't. Sitting in the library, I long no longer for the *Times Literary Supplement*. I want to read Marvel Comics, I want to play in the sand, I want my pacifier back in the mouth where cigarettes now sit, inadequately filling the place of latex or better, a mother's teat. I want to save Jake, I want to save Jake, but first I must save myself.

As the weeks wear on, as the semester unfolds like a disappointingly pale begonia, I become inappropriate in class. In a seminar on aesthetics in a post-Manichean world, the professor whose protégée I've always been says something about the difference between inauthentic and authentic poetry. And I raise my hand only to say, "All the good poets, the real poets, are dead."

The professor looks at me quizzically. Lately Ms. Charney is losing her touch. She hasn't mentioned Plato in four whole weeks and Plato used to dominate her spirited, if disorganized, mind. And isn't it Ms. Charney's place, after all, to remind the dimmer-witted students that Plato also upheld a distinction between genuine and ungenuine art? Foreshadowing Heidegger's differentiation through over two thousand years of thought?

After class, the professor, an object these two years of my literally Platonic love, calls me into his office.

"Ms. Charney," he says, seated at his desk, "is something wrong? Are you having problems getting back into things?"

"Call me Mandy," I say.

"All right. If you wish. Are you having *personal* problems, Mandy?"

"All problems are personal," I say defiantly.

"Of course, Mandy, that's true, isn't it? I know that as well as you do."

"My boyfriend is suicidal," I say. "He's tried to kill himself three times since August. Once, a few weeks ago, he tried to kill both of us."

"Oh my," the professor says.

And then I start to cry. All over his Kierkegaard bibliographies, all over his lecture notes, all over the greatest ideas of our and Everyman's time.

The professor is sympathetic but awkward. He doesn't tell me to read Camus, but neither does he hold me against his intelligent, sturdy frame. He gives me his handkerchief and offers me violet pastilles.

"Remember that T.S. Eliot poem?" I blow my nose loudly. "The one with Grishkin and the feline smell?"

" 'Whispers of Immortality.' " He smiles.

"I love that poem," I say sadly. "You know those last two lines—about not being able to keep your metaphysics warm?"

"Um hum," he says fondly.

"I love those lines," I say. "I'm suffering from—that."

"I understand, Mandy. I really think I do. Forget all this academic work if it doesn't give you comfort. Go outside and look at the trees. You don't have to come to class."

230

"I've always liked you," I say. "As a person, I mean."

"I've always liked *you*, Mandy."

He seems to like saying my name.

"And you know I think you have a very good mind. And I know that when life gets easier again, you'll *enjoy* reading philosophy. Sometimes, it does seem stale. Even art can become irrelevant. There's nothing wrong with that. Art and philosophy will be there when you're ready to come back to them."

"You're being so nice," I say.

"Did you think I *wasn't* kind?" he asks, lowering his glasses onto his nose.

"I knew you were a good person. It's just we never talked before—about real things I mean. . . ."

"We can do more of that, you know. Maybe some day I'll even tell you about my crisis in graduate school. . . ."

"Mr. Haas?" I ask.

"Yes?"

"Do you believe in heaven?"

"I believe in a certain *kind* of heaven—in a mythical sense of belief, of course. Full of Swedenborg's angels. An intellectual's heaven, I guess. I have to go to a department meeting. Will you be all right?"

Jake calls me every day, but doesn't come up to see me. I can't tell if he's actively avoiding me or not, but because I'm not sure I want to see *him*, I don't ask any questions. I extend Mr. Haas's advice to all my classes and don't go to any of them. Mornings I spend sleeping; afternoons I spend meeting the gazes of squirrels; eve-

231

·nings I spend getting stewed with my less angst-ridden friends. The nights I spend alone.

October ends in Halloween, a holiday that's always depressed me. And Jake calls up to tell me he's officially quit school.

"They kept calling me in—to ask why I wasn't going to my classes. And I wouldn't go see my adviser. So today I went and said, 'I quit.' It wasn't like quitting a job, though. I didn't feel good, I felt shitty."

"I feel shitty, too."

"Why?"

"Everything depresses me. I've been drinking a lot. And talking to the squirrels."

"Don't *drink*, Mandy. And don't be depressed. My good news is I got a job. You'll never believe where. I'm working in a cigar factory. I roll the cigars myself."

"That's a good job," I say, meaning it. I don't care anymore about good jobs or bad jobs. I can hardly tell the difference.

"And tomorrow I'm moving into a place on East Eleventh Street. Ninety-five dollars a month."

"You want me to come in and help you?"

"No, I want to surprise you. Fix it up first."

"I want to see you," I say, meaning it.

"The party's in a week. Saturday," he says. "The Greenwald Vulture Party. I'll meet you at Lincoln Center Friday and we can catch a movie."

"Can't you come up here?"

"I'm working," he says, "and I have to move all this shit myself. My parents are giving me all the furniture from the rec room. We'll have a double bed and a couch. It'll be great," he says. "You can *live* here every weekend. It'll be great," he says.

Jake calls me up to tell me he *loves* his apartment. Loves his Ukrainian neighbors and the funny grocery stores. He sounds incredibly cheery, but I don't even realize how bad a sign this is. We don't discuss his health, his moods, his visits to the psychiatrist. He doesn't question me about my black mood either. We are each alone in our pain.

I have stopped nagging him altogether, I don't try to bolster him up, or make rosy claims for our future. And besides, *I'm* the one who needs the bolstering. I cry and drink and have terrible dreams I don't bother to unriddle. Why should I try to save Jake from dying? Now I want to die, too.

In my dream that Wednesday night I am eaten up by a grizzly bear who promises me I'll like it.

Thursday night I go out to a bar with Georgine Martinson and Earl. Earl has brought along a fatuous fraternity brother who marvels at my drinking capacity and talks about his yacht, the *Lacoste*.

As I sink deeper and deeper into a misery that refuses to yield to the comfort of insensate dark, I decide to go off to Manhattan with the fraternity boy named Walt.

Walt is almost comatose when I order my eleventh drink, a sloe gin fizz that proves not slow enough. I pass out in the Rainbow Room, fizzing into a bundle of air which Walt, still the gentleman, spirits off to a taxicab, and later, upstairs to a room in the Howard Johnson Motor Lodge on Eighth and Fifty-first.

JUST AS I SLIDE onto the carpet of the Rainbow Room, downtown on Eleventh off Third Jake eats the last of eighty Elavils, eighty more or less. Nothing particularly painful has happened to him today. He went to work at the cigar factory, joked around with Pancho and Fred, or Tony and Stu, ate a tuna fish sandwich on rye, or maybe it was salmon salad. But he started thinking about Saturday and Mimi Greenwald's party for Leon and Leon's girl. And he started worrying what he'd say to Mimi when she asked him how he was liking school, when she reminded him how expensive N.Y.U. is, what with City College just seven miles uptown and him such a proven dropout. Jake started thinking Ah, what the hell, who cares what the Vulture thinks. Rolling a cigar, he remembers rolling a joint one day in tenth grade.

The air was especially sweet that day, five Octobers ago, and he'd seen Mandy at school, looking sexy in a short white dress. And he'd leaned against her locker, and though he'd never told her—in those days he'd had to fight it—he'd loved her more that day, both of them fifteen years old, leaning up against her locker, than he'd ever, ever loved anyone in his life.

He hasn't smoked pot with Mandy in years. It would be fun to smoke pot with Mandy in his very own apartment and go to the Greenwalds' party high. Mandy would make him laugh and they'd make love again and again. They'd go off to the party, Mandy full of his love and his sperm. And Mandy would protect him from the Vulture. Mandy would make him laugh.

But this stubborn idea won't leave his mind no matter how raunchy are the dirty jokes Paco (or Tony) mutters while the two men sit, one expertly, one just adequately, rolling cigars. And this is the idea Jake can't shake from his mind: Today I do it. Today I'm really going to die.

When work lets up at two-thirty for the afternoon break, Jake takes a subway to Penn Station, hops a train to Bel Ridge, and walks the seven blocks from the station to Ritzler's Family Drugs. He refills his prescription for Elavil and tells them to charge his parents' account. The pharmacist on duty, maybe it is the new guy Frank who doesn't know all the ropes, or maybe it is Mr. or Mrs. Ritzler who should have been more alert, but the pharmacist on duty ignores or doesn't see the special instructions printed in red on Jake's prescription card: This prescription is not to be refilled more frequently than once a month, and then it is to be handed directly to Mr. or Mrs. Rinehart alone. Jacob was not to be handed anything stronger than Aspergum.

Such a nice boy, Mrs. Ritzler might have thought. I've known him since he was a baby.

*   *   *

235

Jake walks then to his family's Colonial house on Pennington Road. He discovers that Girlie, the mutt his parents gave him for his seventh birthday, has wet the carpet again. With Chuck almost ready to go off to college and Louie already a college junior too busy with girls to come home weekends, Jake had Girlie to grow up with, to take on long walks and feed and curb.

And that is one of the reasons Jake has made this trip. He wants to say good-by to his dog. Girlie is getting on now. She is almost fourteen years old, almost ninety-eight in dog years. She is as perky as an old lady can manage, but her bladder has started to leak. Jake grew upset when her leaky bladder had her banished from certain rooms, so he improvised rubber panties for her, buying a pair of yellow ones in the baby department of Ritzler's, then cutting an extra hole for her tail. But the dog despised the feel of wet rubber against dry fur and so the panties were abandoned. And Annette Rinehart, understanding soul, watching the mongrel moan and struggle, saw in this doggy discomfort the discomfort of her own child. In order to keep both dog and boy happy, she decided that Girlie could trail her fluids where ever she wanted from then on, Savonnerie rugs be damned.

Jake takes Girlie for a walk. He runs with her through the neighbor's back lot, the Elavil swaying in his windbreaker pouch. He takes the dog inside and feeds her a lamb chop, and then he gives her some filleted veal. He can't get yelled at for ruining dinner because by then he'll be dead.

Exulting in this idea, the idea he'll be dead by morning, Jake is like a naughty young boy plotting puppy-tail mischief. He takes a second and then a third lamb chop from the Rinehart's busy freezer and leaves them on the counter to defrost.

Upstairs in his bedroom, Jake removes some insurance papers from his surprisingly voluminous files. In the files are love letters Mandy wrote him, an unrequited fifteen. There are newspapers he put together at ten with excerpts from books he liked: *What Makes Sammy Run?*, and later, *Fanny Hill*. In his files are vital statistics on maybe one hundred celebrities: the names of Billie Holiday's lawyers, the telephone number of Woody Allen's first wife, the name of the hotel Jean Shepherd used to stay in whenever he was in St. Louis.

Jake takes out the file marked: IMPORTANT: DO NOT STEEL. (He used to spell words wrong on purpose—it was his most transparent affectation—there *were* things he could not hide.)

But hide, shmide, he is almost dead and the lamb chops are busy defrosting and making the counter wet. Jake takes the papers out of the folder—some stock certificates for I.T.&T., a life insurance policy taken out by his sonless Uncle Bill when Jake was a newborn and happy.

He leaves the papers on his desk, replaces the desk chair neatly.

Jake goes into his parents' bedroom. Everything is lilac and pretty. James Michener's *Hawaii* remains on the nightstand, its backbone bent open at page eighty. He touches the frayed spine of the book and leaves the room to go downstairs.

Downstairs, the lamb chops are still too frozen for the warm muzzle of old Girlie. She is too much the lady to shock with icy lamb. So Jake wraps the chops in aluminum foil, replacing them in the refrigerator, a well-trained suburban son.

I wake up at four-thirty and my guts hurt and I want to throw up. Walt, the fraternity boy, asleep, looks white and puffy in the room's throbbing light. Lights glare everywhere—both night tables, the closet, the bathroom, the foyer, the overhead. What could have been in Walt's mind?

I'm depressed to realize I'm naked, but have no memory at all of whether the tall fraternity boy stuck anything inside me. I'm bruised a bit on one thigh, my head is stuffed thick with mucus, jockey shorts lie neatly folded on a luggage stand. I start crying.

I find my pants and blouse, I stuff my underwear into my purse. I walk, reeling, down the corridor and out of the Howard Johnson's. Downstairs in the lobby, the clerk bothers to ask me, "Is the gig up so soon?"

Outside it's still dark and I take the first cab ride I've taken alone in twenty years to Grand Central. At the station, I want to call someone. But who? Jake doesn't have a phone. And if he did have a phone, I have no way of knowing, he would not be there to answer it. Though Jake isn't dead quite yet.

Down at St. Vincent's Hospital, a fifteen-minute cab ride away from Grand Central, Jake calls the psychiatrist. Philip Nold sits in his shorts at his dusty dining-room table. He's fallen asleep waiting for Jake Rinehart to call him back. A cantaloupe sits in a bowl. Before he was picking at it. Being a doctor is sometimes nice—the money buys cantaloupe in November. But tonight it's a miserable business—the patient he likes the most is dying.

Nold *wants* to go down to the hospital and sit with Jake Rinehart. Maybe he could take the boy to an all-night diner for blintzes. Or sit beside him while he sleeps it all off, the father he's always wanted to be to the son he was never given. But his two motherless girls are sleeping, the maid is visiting a sister in Albany, it's too late in the night to call Roz and ask her to come and sit with the girls. And Jake is his patient, not his son, though now, tonight, he wishes otherwise.

"Dr. Nold? I just had my stomach pumped. I don't feel too good. But I'm going home—to the apartment."

"Stay in the hospital, Jake. You need to be taken care of."

"I signed myself out. I'm over eighteen. I want to go to my place. I'll call you tomorrow."

"Take it easy, Jake. Call me around noon. You have to sleep."

Jake walks back to his place. It is five in the morning and he wishes he were dead.

Turning on the kitchen light, he watches the cockroaches scamper. He doesn't step on the bugs. Instead he feels the queerest urge to get down on his fours and pet one.

Jake looks out the window. And then he bangs his head against the wall. He bangs it gingerly. A lover, not a fighter, he inches up to the wall as close as he can get, and *then* he bangs his head.

Jake leafs through a magazine, *Penthouse* or *New York*. He looks at women's pearly bodies, or else he looks at girls in sweaters and skintight dungarees, girls doing girlish, sophisticated things. He goes into the toilet to examine wine-colored bruises. His face looks really bad. He's not going to the Vulture's party no matter *what* happens.

And yet, as the Fates would have it, the Vulture gets to go to his.

I take the 6:10 train to Bronxville—the first one I can catch. If I tried to call Jake's apartment now—if he had a telephone—I would get to speak to him, to possibly save his life. But I don't want to talk to him anyway. I feel too miserable. It is worse than if I *had* gone to bed with a stranger, straightforwardly and for real. The way things stand, I've no idea what I might have done. And

240

this is infinitely worse. My head is spinning in tortured circles, my hair is matted in the way of the crazy. After a while, the dim-lit suburbs of Mount Vernon come into sight.

Jake lifts back the wooden top that covers the tub and turns on the water. He is going to take a bath. He stands naked above the tub, burly and hairy and five feet five. He readies some reading material—his bathtub has a piece of pine you can prop up to make a table—and then he starts to sweat.

He feels a pressure on his chest—it's like there are people sitting on it. Who *are* these people who sit on his chest, robbing him of air? Is it Dr. Nold? Mimi Greenwald? Is it Chuck or Mandy? Leonard or Mom? Or are they—these squatters—Nazis decked out for full-dress parade? Or are they gang-style Mafiosi flicking dung-colored ashes onto his hairy, heaving chest? Why does it *hurt* so much?

Jake goes to the refrigerator and pours himself some Coke. He arranges magazines on the leaning board, decides to smoke a cigar. He breaks out one of the H. Upmanns Chuck gave him when Garth was born. The cigars are festooned with blue grosgrain ribbon. They are stale, but Jake doesn't notice. *Why does it hurt so much?*

He gets into the bathtub then, but has to get out to find some matches. Feeling kind of queasy then, he leans against the refrigerator before he pours some more Coke.

Back in the bathtub, he sudses his shoulders, takes a

241

sip of the soda and belches. He feels incredibly weak. He is having a heart attack.

I walk from the train station to the campus, the strength draining from my knees. Tomorrow, I promise myself, none of this will matter. Either the preppy boy fell in love with me, suffered the wildest night of his life, or else nothing happened. *So what* if I was seen naked by a naked brother of Alpha Delta Phi? Tomorrow, none of this will matter. Tomorrow I am meeting my Jake, who loves me, at Lincoln Center.

Back on the campus, I find my way to my dorm. With the unnatural instinct of a sleepwalker, I climb the stairs, enter my room, fall asleep on the bed.

By now, Jake is practically dead.

In the bathtub, he starts to pass out. He is reading a magazine article, "Will the Beatles *Really* Get Back Together?," and his vision starts to blank out. He feels so deeply, utterly nauseated that nothing—not Coke— seems to help. The sweating seems to get worse— despite his being in water. The pain has moved from his chest to his shoulders; the pain has moved from shoulder to arm. He feels a sickness in his jaw. He floats. And soon he is floating dead.

I wake up the next afternoon and I am very hung over. My tongue is an orange color I cannot interpret; I

242

feel like I've eaten a roll of gauze. I fill the hall bathtub with sudsy water, pouring in four precious ounces of somebody else's Chanel cologne. One way to get back at the debutantes is to raid their cubbyholes.

Clean and rosy, my skin made rubiate with scalding water, and maybe, new hope, I take some of Georgine's Lemon Body Mist and spray it here and there, all over. I pad back to my room and dress. I want to look pretty for Jake and I have to find something to wear to the party.

I can't find Jake anywhere. Usually we meet at the postcard rack when we meet at Lincoln Center. I look in a few different rooms in the library. I scan the lobbies, I go outside. In the fountain, two boys, their jeans rolled up, are trying to retrieve the pennies.

Finally I call my mother.

"Jake was supposed to meet me here an hour ago."

"Come home," she says.

"I thought maybe he called *you* to say he'd be late."

"Come home, Mandy."

"What's the matter, Ma?"

"Nothing, your father just wants to talk to you."

"I have to wait for Jake. He doesn't have a phone. He said he'd meet me here at five. It's after six. Maybe I should call his mother."

"Don't call his mother."

"Why not? What's going on?"

"Where are you now, dear?" My mother's voice sounds peculiar.

"At the fountain. In front."

"Stay there. We'll come and get you."

"I'll go downtown—to Jake's apartment. Maybe he fell asleep."

"Mandy, listen to me. Stay where you are. Be outside. We're coming. We're on our way."

I sit outside by the fountain. Jake has fallen asleep. Poor Jake. The medicine makes him so tired. Maybe they'll take him off the medicine. . . . But why is my mother so upset? If my father wants to talk to me, *he* can't be dead, right? Maybe Leslie is dead. Maybe Leslie was beat up or raped in Central Park. Maybe my father's dog has died. But Claire is only seven. Claire is too young to be dead.

The boys are laughing and splashing each other. They've given up on the pennies. The November wind carries ice and winter. Aren't they cold with their feet all wet?

My father and mother pull up, and Claire, nestling between them, is barking wildly, alive.

"Is something wrong—is it Leslie?"

"Wait till we get home, Conrad," my mother tries to whisper. My mother's face is blotchy and her voice cracks when she speaks.

"What is it?" I say. "Tell me."

244

"It's about Mr. Jake," my father says. We are stopped at a traffic light.

"He's dead," I say.

"He's dead," my father says.

"I have to go there now," I say. "I have to see Mrs. Rinehart."

"Don't go over there now. She's probably in no mood. They found him themselves—this morning."

"I have to go there," I say. "Who told you he was dead?"

"What's the difference," my mother says. "His uncle. Mandy, try to relax."

"I'm relaxed," I say.

"I'll make you some soup, baby." My mother makes me soup. I look at the soup. It is chicken soup. Bubbles of fat swim on top.

I sit in my parents' room. We watch a made-for-T.V. movie. The main character has just killed her husband and buried him under the barn.

I sleep in my parents' room that night. I sleep on the couch. My mother says if I want to, I can get in the bed with them.

In the morning, Leonard comes over. He has flown in from Los Angeles on the same flight as Louis and Andrea. Leonard tracks dog shit onto the carpet. My mother makes a joke.

Leonard doesn't know what to say. He didn't know Jake was crazy. He didn't know Jake wanted to die. It's my place to reassure him, give comfort, but I don't know what to say either. I think of them, best friends at eight. Two bad boys plotting a way to trick Kerri Mandel into eating doody.

"I remember that time in ninth grade—remember? When you and Jake stole the wheelchair? From the nurse's office? That was the first time I met you. You were wheeling Jake through the halls."

"And Fagioli made us stay after school for a year?" Leonard says.

We sit there smoking cigarettes. For a long time we say nothing. It's too early to start remembering. Leonard cries on and off and on and off I hold him. But I can't cry.

"You going over there?" I ask.

"I was there this morning," Leonard says. "There's a million people there. It made me feel worse. The funeral's tomorrow. Call people up."

"I can't, Leonard. You call people."

"I can't either. But Mrs. Rinehart told me she wants young people there."

"You call young people. I'm going over there now."

"Come over after you see them," Leonard says. Leonard and Jake were neighbors. Leonard lives right around the corner.

The Rineharts' house is full of people I don't know. I sit down in the kitchen with Andrea and Sandy. Louis and Chuck are down at the morgue with Jake.

"Eat a cookie, Mandy," Andrea says.

246

"I don't want a cookie. Why did he have to have an autopsy?"

"There were bruises all over his face. They weren't sure he wasn't mugged."

"I thought he had a heart attack."

"He did, Mandy, but he had these bad bruises. They had to make sure they were—self-inflicted."

I start to laugh hysterically. Imagine getting mugged to death on your way home from trying to kill yourself.

Once somebody had tried to mug Jake late at night in the Village. He had read somewhere that if you act crazy, the mugger might get scared and run off. Jake had started dancing and singing and foaming at the mouth. The mugger had fled into the night. But what if Jake just made that up? What if it never really happened?

Sitting in the Rineharts' kitchen, I am still laughing.

"Are you all right?" Andrea asks.

"I'll give you a Valium," Sandy says.

"I'm all right, but I'll take the Valium. I was just laughing at something funny."

I sneak upstairs to Jake's room. I look inside an ashtray and find a half-smoked cigar, some burnt matches. I empty the contents of the ashtray into my skirt pocket. Annette Rinehart walks in. She looks stunned.

"You want me to leave?" I ask.

"It's okay."

This is the first time we've spoken. When I first arrived she was busy talking to Rabbi Davidowitz. Annette Rinehart goes downstairs, and soon I go down after her.

"I was just in Jake's room. I think Mrs. Rinehart got upset. Does she want me not to go in there?"

"I think she wants the room left alone. Everything just as he left it."

I look at Andrea pleadingly. In my pocket are only ashes.

"Later," she says. "Later. Later, I'm sure she'll let you have anything you want."

THE DAY IS appropriately gray and it's drizzling, on and off. I'm glad it's raining. I want to see umbrellas. Black umbrellas, black limousines, overcast skies—an English thriller. I want it to be like an English thriller. And the hero really isn't dead. He's off on some paradise of an island. Tropical birds, lush palms, native girls shaking heavy breasts.

I put on a skirt of my mother's, a gray golf skirt from the forties. I put on my favorite blue sweater and Leslie's new boots. Something old, something new, something borrowed, something blue.

My mother lifts up my dirty hair and says, "You can't wear this sweater. Look at the size of this hole."

"I want to. It's my favorite sweater. I'll put a pin over the hole."

Inside Leslie's jewelry box I find a pin Jake gave me once, an ink-smeared piece of white tin with red words written across a circle: "Here Comes the Bride." I am a ghosty, witchy woman. I am Miss Havisham. I am waiting for the white boy of my dreams to return and wipe spiderwebs from my hair.

The doorbell rings and Chuck's early. Outside, in the limousine, Sandy and Andrea are crying. Louis has a headache. The driver looks like Sal Mineo.

Inside the small room of the chapel, the coffin is open, and there is Jake. He is wearing a shirt I never liked— apple green—and a figured brown tie. He is wearing *tallis* and *tefillin*. He is wearing a *yarmulka* and much too much foundation. There is makeup stuck in his eyebrows. My finger wants to scretch it out. His grandmother sways over him, praying. "Jeckie," she says, "Jeckie, vake up."

"Jacob," Annette Rinehart whispers. "Baby, Jackie, it's me, Mother. And Mandy is here to see you, too. Mandy is here, your wife."

Louis takes Annette on one arm, Nana on the other. He ushers them to the rear of the room where they sit and shuffle their feet. Nana's eyes roll around.

Sandy and Chuck, Andrea and Louis go into the foyer to greet the mourners. "You keep an eye on *them*, Pop," Chuck says to his father.

"I'm okay," Annette says. "I'm strong as a horse. I'm a horse."

I imagine Annette as a white mare. She whinnies and neighs, whipping her head.

Manny walks up to the coffin and then he starts talking to Jake. Manny sobs uncontrollably, sinks to his knees, rends the air. "I love you, I love you," he says, falling.

". . . Yankev Nahum, Ben Mendel Shlomo . . ." the rabbi speaks with stagy elegance. I notice my father's eyes blinking, he understands these Hebrew words.

The coffin is closed now and inside is Jake. And this is his funeral.

"We cannot," the rabbi says. He clears his throat, begins again. "We cannot judge a life by its length, by its numbered days on this ephemeral earth. We must rather judge it for its quality, the way we choose a good wine."

I think about the rabbi's words as the limousine pulls onto the grass of the cemetery in Queens. The rabbi is riding with us. Large clumps of hair protrude from his nostrils, the nostrils themselves are well-shaped.

"Jacob Rheinbaum was a good man," the rabbi reassures us.

* * *

I see the Thin-Girl-Afraid-of-Everything. She has come to bury Jake, too. It was good of her to come here, she loved him. I feel a charge of sympathy for the crazy young girl who stands there alone.

Soon, before I realize it's time, Chuck throws a ceremonial clump of dirt onto the coffin, and then the gravediggers start lowering Jake into the dirt. The rabbi speaks his nasal Hebrew. Maybe he's really talking gibberish. Leonard breaks his hold on my arm and tries, like a yenta of long ago, to throw himself into the grave. "He's my friend," Leonard says. "They're taking away my friend."

Walking back to Leonard's car, I tell him, "Leonard, he *wanted* to die. You never knew any of it. He was miserable. He tried three times."

"No, Mandy, stop saying it. I *knew* Jake. He was my friend."

As Leonard and I stand in the rain, Mimi Greenwald clicks past us, wobbly on high heels. She is wearing black and gesturing wildly. Her head bobs on an outstretched neck, her arms flap awfully, like wings.

"So I already *have* three pounds of pâté," she tells the woman walking beside her. "I'd already ordered it for Leon's party. I think pâté is nicer than liver, don't you, darling? So, you think three pounds of pâté is enough?"

I look down at my wrist and I notice the stamp on the inside of my arm. The stamp dates back two days ago to my wild night on the town with Walt. We had at some murky point in that evening gone into a discotheque. Walt had told the cab driver to take us to the Rainbow

Room, but the cabbie had misunderstood. When he dropped us at a dancing club, a Latin juice bar, in the east nineties, we had been too polite or too drunk to protest. I had teased Walt into going in and we'd paid the dollar cover charge and had our wrists stamped just in case we wanted to catch some night air on the corner of 101st and Second.

We'd danced one dance, real slow and close, in that other rainbow room, and for a few seconds, it had seemed that I was safe.

I look at the stamp with one eye closed against the sudden sunlight. Has Jake made the rain stop once more, just for me, as a sign? I look down at my sturdy wrist and I watch as the faded inky letters transform themselves into numbers. The numbers shift, then fade just as quickly back into nothingness.

Around me, people are closing umbrellas, chattering over the change in the weather. One old woman, a maiden aunt, wearing nothing but several layers of cardigans, faints into the mud. A gasp goes up among the bereaved, and soon there are no less than six survivors down there in the mud.

They are smoothing and lifting; they are whispering. They are breathing into her ancient face the soothing syllables of life.

ACKNOWLEDGMENTS

All books, and first novels I suppose in particular, begin many years before they begin, and so, then, must the debt of gratitude. To Leonard Bogan, Isadora Castello, Anabelle Cohen, Vincente Cundari, Valerie Horn, Bernice Levine, Alice MacKenzie, Sallie Mellem, William Moore, Sharon Nachimson, John Reid, Marian Shelby and Dorothy Sullivan of the Teaneck, New Jersey, school system, I am grateful for the years of nurturing and inspiration. To Bill Gifford, Jesse Kalin, Michael and Susan Murray, Eric Lindbloom and Nancy Willard, all of Vassar College, I am grateful not only for an education but also for deep generosity during a dark season.

I am deeply grateful to the Stanford Writing Program and all the people connected with it. I owe a particular debt to John L'Heureux, the director of the program, to Dick Scowcroft, the past director, and to Nancy Packer, for their advice, humor, exhortation and friendship. I also thank Dolly Kringel and Carol Simone for helping me through many crazy Palo Alto days.

Dean Crawford, Jeffrey Green, Allan Gurganus, Kathryn Hellerstein, Victor Perera, Emily Raffel and Susan Welch, all dear friends, listened to me read from the manuscript and offered suggestions. I am grateful to Lisane Abraham, Lisa Sheretz and June Flaum Singer for help in preparation of the manuscript.

Bernard J. Denham of the Stanford University Libraries answered many questions about jazz, and my uncle Gary Flaum provided factual information.

I thank all of my students at Stanford University for having shared their secrets with me, as I shared mine with them. Elaine Markson, my literary agent, was wonderfully supportive and wise. Ted Solotaroff gave helpful suggestions and encouragement. Joan Sanger, my editor, and Jill Freeman, her assistant, were extremely helpful in bringing the book to publication.

My parents, Joe and June Singer, and my brother and sisters, Ian, Sharon and Valerie, have been appreciating and editing me since 1952. And to Jerome Badanes I am grateful for the gift of everything—passage, love, into your hands.

Brett Singer
June 6, 1979
Palo Alto, California